CIGAR MONEY

MICHAEL PUTERBAUGH

ACKNOWLEDGMENTS

First and foremost, thank you to the best copyeditor in the business, who happens to be my little sister. Elizabeth Degenhard, without you I would never have been able to do this. Love you.

Thank you to my book designer and publishing consultant, Steven Booth, who expertly guided me through this process.

Thank you to author Paul Levine for taking time out to respond to me and pointing me to Steven. Also, thank you Paul for writing the books you have written.

DEDICATION

This is dedicated to my wife and best friend, Christina.

Family: I am so very fortunate to be a husband, father, father-in-law, grandfather, son, son-in-law, brother, brother-in-law and uncle to an incredible collection of people. Love you all.

And Mom, thank you for instilling in us the love of reading. I inherited your love of silly mysteries, like this one.

CHAPTER ONE

With the front of my pants still all wet, as I watched Marcia across the black wrought-iron table looking down at her food, I was amazed at how attracted I was to her. I seriously believed that this was the only girl I ever truly loved. That passionate, emotional, true love. I still remembered how her hair smelled. I wanted her to say that she was back to be with me, that she had made a huge mistake, and that it was never too late. Instead, she burped.

Less than two short hours ago, I was driving along not thinking of Marcia. I was singing. Singing out loud. "I get my kicks from watchin' people, runnin' to and fro and if you ask them where their goin', half of them don't know. They're the ones who think I'm crazy but they don't realize, that I'm just groovin', groovin' out on life...." I didn't care if people could hear me as I cruised through Canopy Road past the Ritz. I was feelin' great. My '79 Corvette was humming along and I felt good, with the T-Top off, warm shade coming from the overhanging trees. I was late but I wasn't worried. I was groovin', smokin' my cigar, listening to my UB40 cassette, feeling the low gear power of the Corvette and grooving out on life. And yes, it was a UB40 cassette. The car still had the original cassette player and I still had cassettes to play. The shade of Canopy Road ended and I turned right into the bright sunshine onto Fletcher, shifted, and took off toward the Sandy Turtle. The breeze was hot and the ocean to my right was bright blue. I was late but the Turtle would be there, as it had been for the past couple of years.

I shifted down, glided into a right turn, and pulled into the angled parking spot labeled "Reserved for El Jefe." I was "El Jefe." My emergency brake, despite being "fixed" by Beans, didn't work so I put it in reverse, turned the key off and pushed myself up and out of the car.

"Dean," I heard Rose sort of whisper yell. "*Dean!*"

Her voice was coming out of the Turtle, through one of the side windows. We had those sloping shutters that extend away from the windows, that allow a breeze to glide in but that can be pulled shut when a Florida storm comes rolling in off the ocean. I remembered from my childhood that they were called plantation shutters. I couldn't really see Rose's face unless I got up under the slope of the shutters.

"What's up?"

"Hey they some kinda crazy-assed little woman on the front porch wantin' to hunt you down."

"What?"

"Yeah, but she so lit, she be seein' two of you if she see you at all."

"Let me see."

"She ain't got no gun or nothing, 'cause she barely got clothes on."

"All right, let me see."

I continued walking around the Turtle to the big front porch. The porch really was big; we had it built out in front and it extended around the Turtle along most of the other side. You could see the beach from just about anywhere on the porch.

My cigar was to the lip-burning point, so I pitched it. I could see over our low railing but couldn't see anyone on the porch. I came around the front. The salty breeze felt great. I had my usual attire on: jeans, an extremely worn t-shirt, and sandals. I looked at the bright blue of the ocean before turning to the steps. Rose was at the doorway, holding the screen door open, hand on a big hip, pointing to the front corner of the porch, frowning, and saying nothing. I can't remember what step I was on when I saw her. Curled up, asleep in one of the massive rocking chairs we had out there. People drinking at a table at the other end of the porch were laughing and talking loudly, and Bob Marley's "So Much

Trouble" was playing. Man, what an appropriate song. I know Rose didn't time it for that but, man, was it appropriate. "So Much Trouble" could have been Marcia's last name. But it wasn't. It was Hutchinson. Marcia Hutchinson.

I stood at the top of the steps, staring. Old memories . . . well, not really old memories. The memories were recent and frequent, just as they had been constant for all these years. The only girl I thought about often, the only girl I ever thought I truly loved. There had been many girls in my past and women in my present—but none like her.

I shook myself.

"You want me to wake her ass up?"

"Naw, she'll wake up."

I followed Rose back into the Turtle, letting the oversized front screen door slam. We got the oversized screen door for a cheap price; it never really lined up properly and it slammed, even though the frame was really light. I liked it that way. Maurice, on one of his few trips back, bitched about it, but I thought it was kind of distinctive.

The place inside was not crowded but it was early. Another Bob Marley song was on, but I was in a kind of daze, still thinking about Marcia. I could see her through the front windows, still sleeping. We only played reggae music, or a variation of it. My orders. No karaoke, no theme nights, no hard rock, no country, no juke box, no requests (unless it was reggae, or a variation of it). The Sandy Turtle was a casual beach bar. I reached in the metal cooler and pulled out a nonalcoholic beer and took a sip. Non-alcohol was how I'd been since coming back to the beach.

"Hey, Dean, what's up?" It was Sara.

The only waitress working this time of day, Sara was exceptional looking, just recently twenty-one, and partially a great waitress, who did well in the tip department primarily because she was so cute. Cute and bubbly, but lacking somewhat in the memory department. Thankfully, she could make forgetting half an order genuinely cute. She flirted with me a lot, but I knew that being nearly her father's age would make it weird. Plus, I never hooked up with the help, except Rose when she was half the size she was now what seemed like a lifetime ago. It was sort of rule number one, an if-you're-a-drug-dealer-don't-do-your-own-drugs kind of philosophy.

"Sara, how are you?"

"Great," nudging her head toward the door, "Rose said that sleepin' lady wanted to talk with you in the worst way."

"Well, I guess not until she's done sleepin'."

Almost on cue, as I was watching her through one of the big opened front windows, Marcia began to stir. She opened her eyes quickly but moved slowly. She wiped at her mouth and looked around trying to figure out where she was, I guessed. She looked like those people you see at an airport who had awkwardly fallen asleep and then suddenly awakened not knowing where they are. I figured about a minute after she realized she hadn't missed a flight, she'd know where she was.

I walked from around the bar and headed outside. Marcia noticed me when I was at the doorway.

"You come here to return my warm-ups?" Our first year at Pitt, I had given her my favorite set of football warm-ups.

"Oh, Dean, please. . . ."

I stayed a distance away from her. She was tired, had been drinking heavily while at the Turtle, but it was her eyes. Even though I hadn't seen her for so many years, even though she looked older, a bit worn—her eyes jumped out at you. They were a green color that drew you in. To me, she still appeared as the freshman cheerleader I had met at college orientation.

"Oh well, warm-ups aren't really needed here, I guess."

"Can you take me away from here?"

"Yes, hang on." I did want to take her away from there. I wanted to go somewhere with her. Somewhere quiet and cool and just talk with her and hug each other and forget all that happened in the past yet remember all that we had in the past. I wanted to just start again, to just pick up where we left off, to forget the many years that had passed and return to our college days. To be carefree, without problems, just focused on each other. I wanted to take her away, show her the man I had become and learn about the woman she was.

I turned and walked back into the Turtle. I told Rose I was leaving for a little bit.

"A little bit of we knows what." Both she and Sara laughed.

CHAPTER TWO

The best thing we did was hire Rose. I could leave like this and not worry. In the two years Rose had been with us she had come to view the Turtle as her own. Plus, she could intimidate anyone who thought about getting unruly.

I went back out to the porch. Marcia had her back to me facing the ocean, with the sun just barely starting its descent. The breeze was light on her. Man, I liked what I was looking at. She turned quickly when the door slammed behind me. She had reacted more quickly than me and caught me coming out of my transfixed state. I thought, or maybe wished, she smiled a little.

We went down the steps and around the Turtle to my car. I asked her how she got here and she flung her arm up toward a white Volkswagen Beetle parked by the main road. Thankfully there was no lit or recently lit cigar in the miniature flip ashtray of the Corvette. I often left my cigar burning in the ashtray. If I didn't come back soon enough it usually went out. It didn't do a lot for the interior smell of a car but I rarely had the T-Top on, so it thoroughly aired out, leaving no lingering smell.

"Smells like cigars in here," she said as she got in.

She didn't know I was a cigar smoker, which made me realize that she didn't know me.

I started smoking cigars, at least regularly, shortly after joining the Pittsburgh Police Department. That had to have been nearly eighteen years ago.

"Jaime told me you were some kind of security guard, or bouncer, in Pittsburgh."

Aw, Jaime, nice. "Actually, when I left, I was a detective with the Pittsburgh Police Department."

"Jaime . . . he never could remember things correctly. . . ." She said this while staring off, almost under her alcohol breath, sort of dreamily. I know she was thinking of Jaime or his inability to remember things correctly and not about me being a detective when I left.

"How is Jaime?"

She looked at me like I had just accused her of being fat and, at the same time, told her that her dog had died. A strange facial mixture of how dare you and oh no. And then she started crying.

It was becoming painfully clear to me that Marcia hadn't tracked me down to confess her undying love for me and sweep away with me for passionate lovemaking. I couldn't imagine a *Cosmo* article about "How to Win Your Old Flame Back" that would suggest showing up at his place of work and, if he is not there, drinking until you passed out in a chair. I suppose that should have been my first clue. Thinking of Jaime and perhaps realizing that Jaime was still of importance to her changed my attitude. I could feel the pain of her having left me for Jaime. It was though the pain had been uncovered within me. Buried deep in me, like a rock covered in dirt, and she was wiping the dirt off and the rock was becoming exposed.

I hadn't asked her where she wanted to go so instinctively I was headed down Atlantic Avenue toward town. As I shifted into neutral to let the car roll to a red light, I reached behind her seat and pulled out my cigar case. While she was crying a little into her hands, I cut the end off of an Onyx and lit it. She noticed, looked at me, and began wiping the tears from her eyes. We didn't say anything. She opened her little purse and pulled out a pack of cigarettes.

"Are you serious? You're going to smoke a cigarette in here?"

"You're smoking."

Jesus, we were sounding like an old married couple.

"Yeah, but this is a cigar, a fine one at that."

"What's it matter—this car smells like a giant ashtray anyway."

She was right, I suppose.

"True but those things are bad for you."

"Man, Dean, you haven't changed . . . can we just get a drink and somethin' to eat?"

I remembered. She required food about every two hours. Despite being about 5'2" and 110 pounds, it seemed as though she ate all day. I didn't think she needed another drink but I knew where to take her to help her out on the food front.

"Sure."

I continued into town and took a right on 3rd street. Marcia made no comment about the cute little fishing town that was Fernandina Beach. Although I had been to her family's house more than once in Ohio, to my knowledge she had never been here.

I thought the Caribou Café was the perfect place. Light food, shaded courtyard atmosphere and, I knew, at this time in the late afternoon it would not be too busy. We parked diagonally. I left my cigar in the miniature ashtray and she threw her half-smoked cigarette out. Watching her smoke and seeing her throw it away, I didn't believe that she was a smoker.

She was unsteady getting out of the car. I pointed over her shoulder to where we were headed and she turned and started to walk. I couldn't help but watch. She still looked great. Still looked like a cheerleader. If she would have had on a halter top that smashed her boobs, a little tight skirt, and some white Nancy Sinatra boots made for walkin', you would've thought she was a Dallas Cowboy cheerleader. In which case, you probably would have thought what the hell is a Dallas Cowboy cheerleader doing walkin' around Fernandina Beach? Whatever. . . . Her shorts and shirt were appropriate and she wore them very well. I had also noticed that she was not wearing a wedding ring.

I opened the door for Marcia and we entered the café. I guided her with my arm nearly around her waist toward the side of the room that had no wall, that led out to the courtyard. My arm lightly touching on her waist didn't feel out of place; it felt normal and natural and I don't think either of us really noticed. Ginger, the owner, said "Hey, Dean . . . ," stopping when she noticed Marcia.

We continued out to the patio area and took our seats. I was watching Marcia reading the drink menu when the waitress approached over my right shoulder.

"Hi, y'all, my name's Lori and I'll be takin' care of you."

Y'all. Lori. I looked up. Jesus, Lori was a waitress here. Lori and I had had something very recently. The something was intense and physical. But I didn't know that she had left Brett's as their waitress and was now a waitress here.

"Ahhh, Lori, this is Marcia, Marcia—Lori."

They were pleasant toward one another, Marcia not suspecting anything or maybe not caring. She still looked disheveled and I thought it looked pretty clear that she had been crying.

Marcia ordered some type of rum drink and I got my nonalcoholic beer. Lori returned with two glasses of water and the drinks. She gave Marcia her drink and the glass of water. I was thinking how I hoped Marcia would down the water first and dilute the rum thing. Lori placed my beer down and then with a move that had about as much authenticity as a WWE wrestling punch, faked fumbling my glass of water and fired every ounce in a perfect, forceful splash into my crotch. Watching it unfold in a sort of slow-motion realization, I didn't even react. I didn't jump up.; I just looked up at Lori. She was angry and hurt. I felt bad. She just turned and walked off. Ginger came right away and apologized, saying she "doubted" I deserved that, and left us to get me a towel.

"Apparently, your crotch needed to be watered down," Marcia said.

"Yeah, I didn't realize those glasses held that much water."

"Listen, Dean, I don't want to create problems but I didn't know where to turn. I remembered you lived here and I thought I'd take a chance driving up here. You weren't hard to find, I think everyone knows you here . . . you and Maurice."

Ginger brought me a piece of cloth she called a towel; actually it was a tiny washcloth with grease stains on it. I knew whose side she was on. She took our orders and, despite being hesitant to order anything that Lori, and Ginger for that matter, might be able to get their hands on prior to my consumption, I couldn't resist. This place had the best vegetarian food around. In addition to not drinking, I had also become a vegetarian. Well, not a true vegetarian. Living in an ocean town, I still ate seafood.

She had said "driving up here." I knew that Marcia and Jaime had been living somewhere in the Miami/Fort Lauderdale area.

I listened to her, watched her eat little and drink a lot.

Now she burped. It wasn't a loud burp and it wasn't like she burped in my face. Her head was down; she was tired and had been drinking too much. She looked up slowly, with those green eyes.

"Dean, do you have somewhere I can lie down for a little?"

"Sure, Marcia, but do you have somewhere you want me to take you? Home?"

"No, home is far away. I'm from Chagrin Falls, you know that."

"No, no I mean home here, where do you live? Are you living with Jaime still?"

She started crying again.

"I don't know, I don't know where Jaime is, I need you to help me find him, Dean. He hasn't been home."

"OK, where do you guys live?"

"The Lago Mar, Fort Lauderdale."

"OK, well, that's too far for now. Why don't you get some rest at my place—is your car back at the Turtle?"

"What Turtle?"

"My bar, my place."

"Oh yeah, everyone knows the Turtle, and you, and Maurice."

She was deteriorating fast.

"Marcia, let's go."

I stood up and the coldness of the water on the front of my pants made me move in a weird motion. The place had gotten some more customers, tourist types. I took a big step around the side of the table and helped Marcia get up and move to the door. Ginger was coming at us with a tray of food and I asked her if I could just take care of her later, and she said yes.

As we were walking, Marcia sideways, and me trying to hide my crotch area, Lori was standing with a four-woman group near the door. It looked like a mom and a daughter and daughter's friends or something like that, and I heard Lori say loud enough for just about everyone else to hear,

"We had to ask this guy coming toward us and his drunk girlfriend to leave because he wet his pants."

CHAPTER THREE

The drive to my house was very short. It would've been a short walk even. I lived on 4th street. One up from the Caribou Café and a little ways across Atlantic. I lived by myself in a small green house that had a front porch and a small backyard. It had been totally refurbished by the previous owner and was very nice.

I knew it was clean so I didn't have to worry about Marcia thinking me a slob. I, of course, was a slob, but I was also a man who knew his limitations. It never once occurred to me that I could keep a place clean, so I had hired Caridad Aquino, a fine older woman from the Dominican Republic, to clean twice a week. It really didn't need that much cleaning, but Cari did my laundry and liked to work in my tiny garden. I think she enjoyed the break from raising her five kids in nearby Yulee. Cari sometimes called me "El Jefe," hence the "Reserved for El Jefe" at the Turtle. I didn't know if she was "legal" or not, and I didn't care. I figured the INS was busy trying to bust politicians and movie stars for employing "illegal" help and that they would leave me and Cari alone. Knowing I loved polenta, Cari occasionally brought me food; she couldn't understand how I could survive eating just things like "jogert." She had a key to my place, and she'd been there yesterday, so my house would be free from any evidence of slobbiness.

The sun was getting low, there was something of a breeze going on, and Marcia must have been more drunk or tired than I thought because she was nearly asleep, almost as soon as we got in the car.

"OK, Marcia, you and Jaime live at Lago Mar, Fort Lauderdale?"

"Yes."

Well, at least she didn't start crying when I mentioned Jaime.

"How long have you lived there?"

"Dean, I don't know . . . I'm really tired and drunk. I think . . . we moved there from Miami; Jaime wanted to get away from the man."

"The man?" I asked in something of a shocked questioning voice.

"Yeah, you know Whitey. Jaime had it with Whitey."

What the hell? Jaime wasn't black. Neither was Marcia. I had half a mind to bitch slap her. Maurice used to say "whitey" a lot. He told me once I wasn't whitey because he wouldn't be best friends with a whitey.

The Man? Whitey? What was she talking about?

"Marcia, Jaime's not black."

"I never said he was . . . did you think I thought he was black?"

"No, but you said. . . ."

She interrupted, "I don't know why you think that I think that Jaime's black; do you think I'm stupid or somethin', Dean?"

"No, Marcia, listen . . ."

She was fading fast. "I'm trying to but . . . but you need to talk loud, this rattling car sounding thingy is right in my ear," as she leaned her head against the passenger door, "what are you sayin'?"

"Marcia, you said Jaime wanted to get away from the man, whitey—why does he want to get away from the police or whoever?"

We were pulling into my short driveway. Running from the street to just past my front porch, it only really held one car. I had no garage and there was a gate, one of those tall curved things that look like you are entering some kind of rose garden, at the end. Behind that was my yard, which went along the rest of the side of the house and into the back.

She was actually thinking about what I had just said. I literally could see the confusion, the tiny wrinkled forehead.

Then she started laughing.

"No, nooo, not the MAN."

She laughingly slapped me on the upper arm as we sat close in the Corvette. It was a drunken, limp-wristed, easy slap.

"Not the police, silly . . . the MAN is Whitey. Whitey's his name or nickname or something. . . . Whitey's some black guy, they call him Whitey. Maybe he's Puerto Rican or Cuban, I don't know. I never saw Whitey, Dean, I don't know . . . can we go in now?"

She tried but she didn't have the strength or coordination to open the door. I jumped out and went to her side. I helped her out. She couldn't really walk and I couldn't really figure out how to balance her. I stood a second holding her up; she was comfortable being against me, she was little so I just picked her up. Like a groom picks up a bride. It was easy.

"You're so nice, Dean," she said sleepily as I held her, with her head resting on my chest, eyes closed. I stood there longer than I should have hoping my neighbors were not watching. I liked holding her.

I walked easily up to the front door before realizing that my keys were in my front pocket of my jeans. She probably felt like she was on some sort of a fair ride as I had to dip the top half of her body toward the porch floor as I struggled to reach into my pocket. Then I kind of pressed her legs into the door as I fought with the old-fashioned door knob. But I did get it open. My place was cool. Air conditioning plus ceiling fans throughout. It was kind of dark. There were three bedrooms upstairs. Two smaller and mine, which was larger with its own bathroom. When I moved in, I bought everything from catalogs. I furnished everything with indoor and outdoor furniture from Arhaus, Pottery Barn, and Front Gate. I thought I would test the adage "you get what you pay for." After that, when I needed anything, I would just buy locally at garage sales and things.

I carried her straight up the stairs to the guest bedroom to the right. It was nicely furnished, never used, and always cleaned by Cari. I had to give Marcia the fair ride dip again as I pulled the tucked-in sheets free. She made little moaning sounds. I laid her on the bed and removed her sandals. I thought about undressing her, like they do in the movies—when the drunk or passed-out character wakes up to discover their clothes are off and the clothes remover casually appears with a cup of coffee. But Marcia had little on to begin with and I thought she could just sleep fine like that. It was fully dusk now. I turned the shutters a little and pulled the chain on the overhead fan. I looked at her peacefully sleeping there and was brought back to the days when we were young and she was mine. When Maurice would stay away from our dorm room and we would lay in bed with nothing on for hours and listen to the sounds outside. If only you could appreciate things when you have them and not so much after you lose them.

I quickly grew bored sitting on my catalog leather couch downstairs. I got another cigar and was tempted to light it up in the house. I knew Cari wouldn't be back for days so I could probably get away with it. Even though Cari was Dominican, she hated the smell, even the remnants of it. One time I made the mistake of leaving a half-smoked cigar in the kitchen, in a makeshift plate of an ashtray. You would have thought I left a dead mouse on that plate. She carried it out to the back porch at arm's length and as far away from her face as possible, all the while with a pained expression. Now I know someone's soggy-ended, half-smoked cigar is not a thing of beauty but I didn't think I deserved the lecture about how "jou're going to ruin jour house."

So I thought I should get back to the Turtle. Marcia would be sleeping for a while. I was sure of that. I left a small trash can beside her bed, just in case, and wrote her a short note giving her the phone number for the Turtle. In addition to not drinking anymore, becoming a vegetarian, wearing jeans and t-shirts, and listening to reggae music, I gave up having a cell phone. New me.

It was cooling down as the sun was just about gone. I drove back down Atlantic toward the ocean and the Turtle. The Turtle was straight ahead, Atlantic ended at Fletcher and the Turtle was on that corner. As you approached the Turtle, even from a distance on Atlantic, you saw the ocean behind it. With nothing but parking between me and Larry's place, there is a big opening creating the ocean view. Nothing but ocean beyond.

Maurice and I got lucky when we bought the Sandy Turtle. Many years ago, it had been the Conch House. It was a large house that had been an original beachfront home. Way back when, it was owned by an old African American couple, William and Louise Robinson. Miss Louise made the best conch chowder ever known, according to those who tasted her conch chowder. Old Bill told some great stories, based on a little bit of truth, and he made very attractive fishing lures. The demand for Miss Louise's chowder ultimately caused them to convert their house into a shack of a restaurant. It did well, but they got old and, despite having many children, apparently the conch-making trait didn't pass on and for sure the hard working trait didn't, so there was no one who wanted to carry on the Conch Shack business. When Miss Louise and Old Bill died, within days of each other (people believed he died from lack of chowder), the kids had one last chowder bash and closed the doors. They could never decide what to do with the place.

The property wasn't big enough for big-time investors and the kids were very much split on how to proceed. Enter Maurice and me. Maurice, after finishing third in the Heisman Trophy race and then eight years in the NFL, had become a force of a character actor in Hollywood. It was my idea, but our offer price became right when Maurice dangled Hollywood stardom in the face of James, the youngest of the Robinson kids. We grew up with James and we knew the opinion he held of himself. He was made for Hollywood, not running a chowder shack, making lures and talking about how things used to be. So Maurice threw in an acting role in Maurice's latest movie, with actual speaking lines no less. Well, if you consider "here they come" actual lines. But James was confident and sure that if someone in Hollywood heard him say "here they come," then it was just a matter of choosing what parts to play in the future. Hell, if Maurice could do it, anyone could. James talked the rest of the family into selling the shack by promising he'd not leave them behind when he made it big and reminding them, besides, that Maurice and I were like family.

Maurice had the juice to get it done, James had his speaking part and name on the credits, we paid them a fair price, and we honored Miss Louise and Old Bill by displaying black and white photos of them throughout the joint.

I pulled up. My spot was open, as I think people feared whoever or whatever "El Jefe" was and respected the fact that "El Jefe" had a reserved spot. The reggae had been turned up a notch, Burning Spear was playing, and I could feel and hear that there were more people as I turned the corner of the porch. As I walked up the steps, I looked to the chair Marcia had been in—no sleeping beauties this time.

CHAPTER FOUR

There was a nice mix of the some of our usuals and some tourist types. The Ritz Carlton was a midrange walk down the beach and we could count on that, providing people wanted to shake the formality of the Ritz. It was mostly a younger crowd. Jerry was at the bar, seated at the corner where he usually was. Jerry was our version of Norm from *Cheers*. Only his drink wasn't beer; it was vodka martinis. He was not that overweight, and in his mid-sixties but looking and acting like a much younger guy. Jerry was some kind of retail marketer for Winn-Dixie. He was semi-retired, gold chained, used to be a ladies' man but was still appealing to ladies who used to be targets of ladies' men. He had the gift of gab from years of business deals over martinis. He talked a lot and actually said little that made sense. He once told me, "Dean, I could not partially agree with you more." My favorite, which I have even written down to try to figure out was, "Yes, it is certainly remotely and diametrically opposite of touching the body." I haven't been able to decipher it yet and unfortunately I forget the subject matter, which may have been a helpful clue in trying to determine what Jerry was talking about. He was now talking to Rose, who was behind the bar. I went behind, said hi to Rose and Jerry, and told Rose she could take off whenever she wanted. She had opened for me earlier in the day since I knew I would be at Beans's place for a while.

I usually opened. It was my favorite part of the day. I'd come in, no set time, well ahead of when I knew anyone would be up suspecting a bar to be open. I don't like using the term "bar," as in "I own a bar." I usually tell people I own a little reggae bar. I used to say "little reggae place" but that almost always ended up in my having to explain what a little reggae place was. I guess there is no way to describe a bar without saying "bar." Anyway, I get there when the sun is still rising, the waves just sort of lazily slapping against the beach. As if it is something they have to do but they are still waking up as well and moving slow. I open the doors and windows, don't even play music, and straighten up while my coffee brews. The basking of the sun is warm and even and the seagulls are the only consistent sound. I can sit on the porch with a cup of coffee, rock in Marcia's sleeping chair, and reflect upon whatever I choose to reflect upon. Larry across the way doesn't start fighting with his old-fashioned metal trash cans till later in the morning, getting his pizza shop ready for the lunch crowd and orders.

Larry Penso's Pizza has the best pizza around. Rose was his longtime employee before we came; she worked there forever, learning all the secrets of the old Italian. The timing was perfect for Maurice and me when Rose and Larry got in a fight to end all fights. I had been running the Turtle by myself for about a year when Rose came over and asked for a job. I didn't witness the fight to end all fights; I can only imagine and Rose has never told me about it. I discussed hiring Rose with Maurice. We knew no one worked harder, and we knew we could trust her. We also knew that I was near the end of running the place myself and that we'd be looking for someone to help soon enough. After assuring us she was done with Larry, we offered her the position of manager of the Sandy Turtle, with all its accompanying headaches. Of course, we offered to overpay her. Larry couldn't forgive, though. I liked Larry and went to explain to him our hiring of Rose. I told him that we were not in the food business and would never take advantage of Rose's knowledge of Larry's business. Pointing to the Turtle, Larry told me that if I sided with her, Rose no longer was a name to him, and our business together was done. Since Larry never came to my place to listen to music and never bought alcohol from me, I assumed this meant that I was no longer welcome to order pizza from him. This was, in fact, a penalty, and he knew it. I loved his pizza. It didn't take me long to start ordering through a third person, usually Beans. So, from then on, whenever I saw Larry fighting with his old-fashioned metal trash cans, I waved and he flipped me off.

Tonight, Rose hung out a little bit to make sure we didn't get too crowded. Being a weeknight, Sara was the only waitress. When Sara was the only waitress, either Rose or I would occasionally step out from behind the bar and take some orders if things got tight. But, tonight wasn't busy and Sara was doing fine, smiling and coming back to the bar to pick up whatever drinks she had forgotten to place orders for in the first place.

I was thinking about Marcia almost nonstop. Rose pulled me near the end of the bar and, very seriously, in a quiet voice, asked if I was doing OK. I told her I was and that Marcia was so drunk that she was now just sleeping it off at my house.

"You wanna talk it out, Dean?" Rose asked.

"Naw, I'm good, but thanks, Rose."

She leaned up and gave me a kiss on the check.

"OK, then don't worry about, just hit it in the morning; you'll get some," and she laughed as she started walking away.

"Hey, Dean."

It was Jerry. He had been without someone to talk to for a couple of minutes and could take it no longer.

Very upbeat, I walked toward him. "What's up, Jerry?"

"Dean, I was thinking about those guys that were in here the other night."

I knew what he was talking about. Some younger guys had been in and found out that I had played for the Steelers. They were Browns fans but it ended up fine. I am used to it.

"That one guy, the guy that did all the talking, the best way, Dean, to deal with those kinds of guys is to be diplomatically blunt with them like you were. You couldn't have handled that any better."

Well, it was nice to know that I had mastered being diplomatically blunt.

Fortunately, the rest of the night didn't require me to make use of my diplomatic bluntness skills. Jerry just hung around for a little while longer. I think he preferred flirting with Rose over trying to get me involved in a conversation when I was clearly deeply in Marcia thought mode. I closed up around 1:00 a.m. We had no real set hours, no sign about opening and closing, and I would tell whoever was hanging on in plenty of time about when I was going to call it. I'd give them a little "we close at . . ." whatever hour I wanted to shoot for. That night it was 1:00 a.m. and I got no complaint from the remaining two couples. Sara had left around 11:00 p.m. She gets tired early and quickly. One minute she's bouncing around, retaining about half the orders given her, and the next she's sitting on a corner stool looking like she just ran a half marathon.

When I unlocked the door and went into my house, everything was the same as I had left it. Rather than yell "Honey, I'm home," I just walked quietly upstairs and checked in on Marcia. She was sound asleep. I was tired so I went to my room. As I was changing, I was thankful I got in my three-mile run around downtown today. I tried to run at least three miles every other day. I entered nearby 5K races when I could and lifted weights fairly often, forcing myself to do some ab work. I really wasn't changing, just stripping down to my boxers. I was hoping that at some point, during the night, Marcia would slide in between my covers and we would be back in our freshman year at Pitt.

CHAPTER FIVE

No in-between-the-sheet-sliding took place and I slept very soundly. I always sleep soundly. I could be finishing a Starbuck's Venti coffee of the day as I am turning down the sheets, receiving a call informing me that I was a victim of identity theft and my bank account was wiped out, and I would still sleep soundly. So the sleeping soundly part did not surprise me. What did surprise me was that it was nearly 7:00 a.m. when I woke.

Usually I'm up between 6:00 and 6:30. I put on a pair of large gym shorts and a t-shirt and went into the bathroom. In the hallway, I heard nothing but the ceiling fans. No sign that Marcia had gotten up yet. I took my time going to the bathroom and brushing my teeth. As I walked down the hallway, I was debating whether to just head downstairs and start trying to make an impressive breakfast but since I knew I wouldn't be able to make an impressive breakfast and because I really wanted to see her, I decided to go into her room. I honestly thought she was in there until I was about halfway across the room.

There was no sign she had left, other than she wasn't there. I went out on the back porch, surveyed my small backyard, went out on the front porch, looked up and down the street. My car was still there. In the kitchen, no pans or cups had been used. But still something seemed out of place. I concentrated while looking around. Then I noticed it wasn't there. My bike. My bike that I kept behind the sort of two-person chair in the living room. Jesus, she took my bike. How was she riding my bike? That was a big-assed bike. I'm 6'4" and the seat is set for that height. If she was riding it, she was not sitting on the seat.

I got my keys and went to my car. As I drove down Atlantic, I slowed at each side street to look both ways. Like you do when you go out in your car looking for a lost dog. I thought I'd head toward the Turtle because I could not think of any other direction that she would head. Nothing on the side streets. Then I saw the yellow of Butch's bike way down 8th street. I took a wide right turn and headed for it. Fortunately, Butch was in no hurry anywhere this morning. Butch was never in a hurry anywhere. He was of an indeterminate age and mentally a bit slow and his sole purpose in life seemed to be to ride his big yellow Schwinn bike around town telling bad knock-knock jokes. He was basically riding in a huge circle in the early morning empty street. I drove the street to where he was.

"Hey, Butch."

"Mornin', Dean."

"Butch, did you see a woman ridin' my bike?"

Butch knew my bike. He had seen me riding it fairly often and he liked it.

"Yes, Dean, that bike too big."

"I know, Butch, where did she go?"

"She don't know how to go to Turtle."

"Oh, did she ask you how to get to the Turtle?"

"She don't know how to get to Turtle, Dean."

"I know, Butch, thanks," and I drove off. I went back onto Atlantic as I figured she would take that main road to the Turtle. But, nothing. I got to the Turtle and parked my car. I wasn't dressed how I wanted to be, but I got out and went up on the front porch and there it was. My bike was leaning against the window beside the front door. Nothing else, nothing unusual, just my bike leaning against the window. I went back down the steps, from where I had just come, to look for the white Beetle, but it was gone. I looked around, the sun was starting to get strong, the beach was starting to move with activity, but there was no sign of her. I knew she wasn't in the Turtle, because I had locked it up last night. I unlocked the door and headed in. It always felt the same heading in at this time of day. Quiet, dark, and bar-smelling. I had a routine. Leave the front door open, get the ceiling fans turned on, open the windows, and start the coffee. I didn't vary from this routine. With my cup, I went back out onto the shade of the porch.

I didn't know what to do. I sat in one of our big rocking chairs and listened to the birds and the waves. It was getting hot already. The sky was clear and there was activity on the beach. People spread apart by distances but each doing something. I thought about Marcia. What was the point? Why did she appear here? Why did she seek me out? About all I knew was that she and Jaime lived at the Lago Mar in Fort Lauderdale, that Jaime was trying to get away from Whitey, who was either black or Puerto Rican. Beyond that, I didn't know much. I couldn't shake the feeling that Marcia had come to me for help and that, for some reason, I expected it of myself to help her. I was no fan of Jaime and I had lived without either one of them for many years, that was true, but I still thought I needed to do something. She came here for a reason and I don't believe it was to start a relationship. It was for help. I could feel that something was wrong with Jaime and Marcia must have been feeling the same. Maybe more. I am a believer in woman's intuition. Something that would make Marcia seek me out.

I couldn't sit there anymore. Sure, I had mastered the art of leisure and the leisurely lifestyle, but this was stirring me. All of a sudden, it hit me that I had to help her out. That I had to go to her rescue. If a white horse went trotting by at that moment, I would have jumped off the Turtle's front porch railing onto it and rode it all the way down the coast to Fort Lauderdale. Fortunately, no white horse happened to be trotting by so I didn't have to risk smashing my balls jumping onto a bare horseback. But my white Corvette was sitting at the side of my place and I thought about just jumping in and going the distance. Then I remembered all the mechanical problems that Beans worked on that still remained. I wheeled my bike into the Turtle and called Rose's phone. She didn't answer so I left her a message that I was going to Fort Lauderdale and told her that she could open and close the Turtle as she wished. We had no beer deliveries today, so no real commitments. I turned off the coffee and the lights but kept the ceiling fans going and the windows open. I knew Rose would be in soon.

I didn't exactly jump off the porch and into my car and peel outta there. In fact, I was moving slow, thinking about how I was going to get to Fort Lauderdale, the roughly five and a half hours down 95. The day was cloudless and getting hot. I drove my path from the Turtle to my house with the feel of the morning warmth and with the activity of the little town beginning to move.

I took my time in the house as well. I felt I needed to think, so I lit up an Onyx and put some reggaeton music on. I wanted the upbeatness. I felt as though I was going on a road trip. My thought pattern easing from a "I have to save Marcia" feeling of urgency to a "I'm going to go check out Fort Lauderdale" feeling. I knew Fort Lauderdale fairly well. I even knew the vicinity of the Lago Mar. Back in the day, Maurice and I took some road trips there and one time Beans came with us. But I was thinking the Lago Mar was simply an upscale hotel. I was not aware that people actually lived there, and I was fairly certain Marcia had said they were living there. I packed my attaché case with bathroom necessities and threw a couple of days' worth of clothes in my Pitt duffel bag. I took some exercising clothes just in case I was there a couple days, along with a swimsuit. I had a travel case for my cigars and lined up enough in there to last a week. I called Beans at his shop. After many rings, he answered.

"Beans," childhood friend and semi-successful mechanic but mostly a master of flatulence.

Beans rips 'em whenever he wants and in front of whoever he wants to. I learned that in the sixth grade, the first day of Mrs. Henning's class. He ripped one right when she started in, in her old high-pitched voice. She was at the blackboard with her back toward us, having just finished writing her name in fancy cursive chalk, when she turned to pronounce her name and Brian "Beans" Luber ripped the first of thousands that I would hear up to that day in the garage. I could tell Mrs. Henning had been there before because she just took in a heavy breath, causing her huge waist-level old lady boobs to rise up, and she walked over to the front drawer on her desk. Without speaking, she pulled out her ruler and walked over to Beans's desk.

Beans looked up at her and casually said in his southern drawl, "Aw, Mrs. Henning, you ain't goin' to be able to measure that one with a ruler." It was the first time I had seen a ruler used on knuckles.

"Beans, I need to drive down to Fort Lauderdale."

"Well, I hope you ain't planning on that 'vette g'tting' you there."

"No, Beans, of course not. I haven't had that car checked out by a real mechanic for years."

"Haha, I was thinkin' just the other day that this island needs a place you can to and get a drink that isn't watered down and listen to some good old country music."

"OK, Slim Pickens, enough—what can we do to get me a car?"

"Man, Dean, the only thing I got is Lisa's Thing."

"Wow, will that Thing even make it?" The Thing was actually a "Thing." Made by Volkswagen sometime in the 1970s, it was like a cheap Jeep. Lisa, in addition to probably holding the Guinness World Record for one person inhaling and/or hearing human farts, was Beans's wife (thus her claim to the World Record if she chose). Lisa was also a hippy by nature. She'd had Beans paint the Thing a bright yellow with a huge flower on the hood.

"Hell yeah, I put a new engine in it a couple of years ago, the Thing actually hauls ass. It can even haul your big ass to Fort Lauderdale and back. Lisa won't mind; she's into biking and rollerblading or whatever else you can do to get around without polluting our sensitive locale."

"OK, I'll stop by and trade you cars, in a little."

The white horse urgency was completely gone, and I was just sort of lazily walking around the house with that "I'm forgetting something" feeling. I wrote Cari a note saying that I might be gone for a couple days. After convincing myself I hadn't forgotten anything, I locked up, got more than enough money from my hidden stash, and headed to Beans's place. Within the hour, I was cruising in the Thing down A1A toward St. Augustine. I decided to take the back way as it was much more scenic. Driving through the Little Talbot Island State Park with its marshy scenery was something I didn't do enough and I wanted to stop at the Manatee Café just north of St. Augustine for a late breakfast. I timed the ferry ride perfectly and cruised across the river watching dolphins jumping alongside the ferry. It felt sort of liberating, feeling the sun and not having anything responsible to do that day. I knew Rose had it under control. I always liked situations where I knew no one knew exactly where I was. Most people didn't even know I was driving a Thing, let alone driving A1A toward 95 enjoying the views.

The Thing had a canvas-type top but no windows so my ride was feeling very open-aired, warm and breezy, and upon my discovery back at Beans's place that the Thing had a cassette player like my Corvette, I had grabbed my cassette case from my Corvette before jumping in the Thing. With a plentiful stash of cash, cigars, and cassettes, I was moving along.

I crossed the bridge with various white sailboats gliding along the calm waters on the edge of St. Augustine. It wasn't particularly busy at this time and, although nothing near the laidback vibe of Fernandina, it had a smooth quiet about it. The Manatee Café was as I remembered. I resisted the Chocolate Tofu Pie only because I was too full from the Scrambled Tofu and Banana Smoothie breakfast.

Slowly, I walked out to the Thing while cutting my cigar. I stopped while retrieving my Norman Rockwell Umpire painting Zippo from my front jeans pocket. As I was lighting the cigar, I noticed several college-aged kids admiring the Thing. They appeared to be surfer types and I assumed they went to Flagler College.

As I got close, one of the boys said, "Man, this is awesome."

"Thanks," I said. "It's fun."

I heard him saying, "See man, this is what we need," as I was opening the half-metal door and climbing in. I started it up as Omega was cranking out a song and drove away.

CHAPTER SIX

I decided not to hang around St. Augustine and just continue to Fort Lauderdale. My drive the rest of the way was uneventful. I managed to restrain myself to the one cigar for the roughly five hours. I did go through a small patch of afternoon Florida showers but as I pulled into Fort Lauderdale the early evening was hot and clear. The ocean was providing a great warm breeze. I made my way down the strip with the wide, expansive ocean directly to my left. I seemed to remember that the Lago Mar was way down at the end of the strip and, being a typical American male, I thought I would continue without asking directions. Turning left through a neighborhood, I thought I had made a mistake when the street ended, but when I turned right it led me over a little bridge, and as I was on top of that bridge, looking left, I saw the Lago Mar. It appeared from a distance as a grand, white, time-gone-by hotel. The front was facing me. I slowed to a stop atop the little bridge and just observed. There was a body of water, the "Lago" in "Lago Mar," separating me from the hotel. The hotel appeared beautiful to me. The memory of it was coming back. I had last seen it at night, when it was lit up, and I remembered it was beautiful enough then, when I was a drunken teen, enough for a drunken teen to even notice its beauty and be stopped for a moment. That memory stayed with me so, in a sense, this was like pulling out an old, creased postcard from the bottom of a desk drawer. I wasn't able to pull out any further memories because I happened to look up in my rearview mirror and notice a nice old man sitting in his Buick behind me waiting patiently for me to continue my driving. He must have been used to people stopping for this view, because he didn't honk his horn; he just waited patiently. I thought it a shame that we have to think niceness is unusual.

I put the Thing into gear, gave him a wave and a smile, and continued forward. I rounded a bend to the left and saw several high-rises. Some had gates and I began to worry that the Lago Mar may not be a public place, like seemingly everything else nowadays, that it might restrict non-gate-opening visitors. The high rises, although updated, still emitted a seventies feel. Very James Bondish, like in the beginning of *Goldfinger*.

I rounded left again and saw the drive leading up to the entrance of the Lago Mar. On my left was the Lago, on whose other side I had been moments ago. On my right was a three-level white building of condos. I cruised slowly past them and drove up the slight incline to the covered front entrance to the hotel. I looked across the wide expanse of the lake and could pick out the little bridge I had just been on. I pulled up and stopped and a valet in uniform came out to open my half-metal door.

"Good evening, Sir. . . . Reservations for this evening?"

He was a young, wiry kid and he seemed to be eyeing the oddity of the Thing. I could feel that he wanted to jump in it and give it a drive. I was thinking that probably the only real eventful aspect of being a valet was in the kind of car you got to drive off in.

"No, not yet, I'm hoping you have something available."

"Ah, yessir, I am sure we can take care of you," he said and proceeded to lead me through the front doors.

Inside, the lobby had a huge ceiling and floors of some sort of marble. It was air-conditioned and surprisingly dark. The seventies feel that I had felt from the nearby high rises was even more prevalent here. This place was defiantly, yet elegantly, being drug into the modern day. I half expected to see a young Burt Reynolds, with Dom DeLuise tagging along, or the original cast of *Charlie's Angels* come walking through the lobby.

The wiry boy stood off to the side as I approached the front desk. There was no activity, no phones ringing, no people waiting impatiently with suitcases, no kids running around the lobby. Almost instantly, a striking young woman came out of the room and asked to help. I told her that I needed a room and that I might be several nights but that I was not sure. That was not a problem. I asked her if anyone "lived" here, as Marcia had slurred to me, in the Caribou Café, that she and Jaime "lived" at the Lago Mar. She told me that no one actually lived in the hotel but that the three-story white condos immediately next door were called Lago Mar Place and were associated with the hotel and that most of those units had year-round residents.

I gave her my only credit card (that I never used) to secure the room. I decided on a pool-view room instead of ocean view.

Her beauty and her slight Hispanic accent were mesmerizing me until she said, "Joey, can you provide assistance to Mr. Hunter?"

The wiry boy said, "If you want to give me your keys, I can park that car."

"Sure, I'll walk out with you," I said.

The Hispanic beauty gave me an actual key and told me that Joey would show me where the room was after he parked my car.

I walked out with Joey into the early evening warmth where the Thing was. I gave him the key, complete with the big pink PowderPuff Girl key chain. He looked at it but skipped off to the car. As he was starting it up, I reached in the back and grabbed my bag just as he peeled off.

I waited for him because I didn't know where my room was. In a couple minutes he came jogging back.

"Man, I love that car; it's got some balls…. I mean it seems like it can take off, sir."

"Haha, that's OK, yeah it can."

"I'll show you the room. Here are your car keys; it's just parked out front, down the row."

We walked back into the lobby. I was carrying my own bag until the Hispanic beauty behind the desk noticed, frowned at Joey, and angrily tilted her head toward my bag.

"Oh, let me get your bag . . . sir."

"No, it's all right, I got it," I was about twice the size of Joey and I would not have felt right him carrying my bag. I never could handle little caddies carrying my golf bag when I played golf with Michelle's father at his fancy-assed country club. I would carry my own bag and the caddy would just follow and balance it propped up when I hit my shot. I guess it didn't appear that weird since I was about 275 pounds at that time and Michelle's dad made sure everyone at the club knew I played for the Steelers.

Joey and I walked out into a huge pool area with palm trees, chairs, and a lot of activity. The pool seemed to wind around and there was a cement path out to the beach. It was the biggest beach I had ever seen; the ocean was far away. The whole feel was very comfortable. There was a tiki hut bar/restaurant thing in the center that the pool sort of wound around. Joey explained that I was on the second floor and asked if I preferred the elevator or steps. I said steps were fine and he said that was good because the elevators were incredibly slow.

Joey opened my door and I was very surprised by how spacious it was. The seventies was still the era but the room was very clean. I walked in and noticed a balcony that looked out onto the pool and a room containing a king-sized bed through some French doors. I gave Joey a five and he told me he was around all the time and easy to find if I needed him. I was really liking this place. I stood out on the balcony and looked around. The beach and ocean were off to my right and within my view. Straight ahead was the pool and across the pool were the other rooms in the hotel. The pool was very large, and there was sand everywhere else. I envisioned that, in the 1970s, this place was probably a haven for stars seeking a quiet getaway with their sunglasses, white towels and robes, cigarettes, and mixed drinks. The seventies elegance was now home to middle-class families with kids running around everywhere.

I unpacked my things, located the safe and reset the numbers, and put the majority of my cash in there. The air conditioning combined with the breeze blowing in from the balcony and the distant noises of children's voices and splashing had me tempted to take a nap, but I resisted.

Downstairs I located the restaurant. It was a glassed-in, carpeted banquet room with round tables that I am sure had hosted its share of upscale wedding receptions. The bar, off to the side, was dark and contained some dinner booths. I noticed autographed pictures of Chris Evert, Jimmy Conners, Joe Namath, and a bunch of others, even Burt Reynolds, but I could not find a Dom DeLuise.

I did the head nod to the bored-looking bartender but didn't stay. I went out through the lobby, out the front doors, and into the setting sun. I was facing the lake, and the sun was strong but fading. It seemed to me that when it went down the evening air would seem cool and crisp, but for now it was very warming. I walked left, through sort of a shaded corridor that bypassed the lobby and led to the side of the front of the hotel. There was no real sidewalk; I walked on the blacktop toward the Lago Mar condos. They were very close and seemed almost to be a part of the hotel. There were some cars parked in the very limited spaces right in front of the entrance. Marcia's car was not there. I had no idea if Jaime's car was there. I looked for any telltale signs on the cars that were there, like a Pitt sticker or a "I love

Chagrin Falls," but there was nothing but Florida license plates.

There was no real entrance or lobby, just a stairway on either end and two elevators in the middle. I looked for a directory but couldn't find anything. The stairway and elevators appeared to lead to balconies that ran around the exterior of floors two and three. It was much like an old motel building, except all white and very clean. There was no one around and it was very quiet. I decided to walk around the side of the building that was closest to the hotel. The side of the building had very green, almost plastic-looking bushes and grass all along the wall and was shaded. The bushes continued beyond the end of the side of the building and tapered off to the left to connect with the hotel shrubbery. In effect I was trapped at the V by the Hotel bushes on one side and the condo bushes on the other. The condos had a nice-sized pool of their own, the hotel and condo pools connected by a cement walkway. Several people from each side just looked at me like you would look at a person who was in a place that he was not supposed to be. I walked back and decided that I would just walk from my hotel pool to the condo pool. I made my trek back to my hotel.

I walked through the cool marble lobby, down the hall, and out the glass doors. Instantly the contrast was almost shocking. I had been in a dimly lit marble hallway with no one around, a sophisticated silence of high walls and little lighting. But when I opened that door it was fading sunshine, water splashing, the noise of children, and the smell of chlorine. The contrast was telling. I knew this had been a place of quiet, sophisticated silence that catered to celebrities about forty years ago but that now it was where young parents brought their children and felt comfortable leaving them to entertain themselves in the massive winding pool and sandy areas under the palm trees while they sipped on their fruited drinks. The remnants remained, but much like America everything was seemingly less formal and more family focused.

I went to the outside tiki hut bar and surprisingly learned that they offered a soy burger on whole wheat bread, no less, and nonalcoholic beer. So that was my order. I walked from the hotel pool to the condo's pool while my food was being made. There was no obstruction, no real divider other than the bushes, and the two people at the condo pool barely glanced at me. I looked at each unit on the three floors of the stark white U-shaped building. I couldn't detect anything that would lead me to believe one unit over another was that of Jaime and Marcia's. After a sufficient amount of observance time, I left to go check on my food.

Eating at a table in the sand under the cool shade of a palm, I watched three kids play a form of chess with hotel-supplied pieces that were bigger than each of them. I finished the rest of the sunlight off by walking on the beach, smoking a cigar, and thinking of Marcia, Marcia and Jaime, and Marcia. How my life may have been different if I had ended up with her and how her life may have been different. I somehow felt that hers would have been more stable. That life with Jaime was probably a wild ride. Then I realized life with me probably wouldn't have been much of a picnic.

CHAPTER SEVEN

I noticed Marcia right away at freshman orientation at Pitt. It was almost as if my eyes were drawn directly to her standing across the room. We had started dating instantly and intently soon after that orientation. The big football player and the little cheerleader. I can't remember when she met Jaime Devine; I don't even know who introduced them before I did or if they met the way football players and cheerleaders sometimes meet, but by the end of our sophomore year she was gone with him. Jaime was from Pittsburgh, a local private high school star quarterback who had accepted a scholarship to play for the local university. A quarterback. I hated quarterbacks. He was everything that a star quarterback should be: good-looking, athletic, from a wealthy country club family from the Squirrel Hill area of Pittsburgh. I do remember the first time I saw them look at each other.

It was at a house party, near the end of our sophomore year. I was with Marcia. Marcia and I were together a lot. This night, I had been drinking a lot of beer and Marcia hadn't. Jaime appeared with Michelle, his girlfriend at the time. They just appeared by our sides. Over the blasting music I yelled out the introduction of "Marcia this is Jaime, Jaime this is Marcia." I half expected the music to transition from blasting crap house party music to a single harp and for little blue cartoon birds to start flying around their heads as they looked intently at one another and shyly admitted that they had met. Jaime, remembering he was with Michelle, introduced us. I thought Michelle looked out of place at this party but beautiful. I suppose it was the alcohol, my awareness of Marcia and Jaime's love at first sight—or second sight or however many sights—or maybe it was the newness of Michelle that caused me to pay too much attention to her, but the flow was set. Me, drinking beer, loudly high-fiving other football players and being too interested in Michelle, Michelle trying to watch over her prize quarterback boyfriend from high school, Jaime trying to balance the interest of and in the two, and Marcia drawing Jaime in with her eyes.

After that house party, Marcia and I had gotten in a fight. Looking back, as I had on many occasions, I believe that Marcia started it on purpose and I was too drunk to know better and just reacted by fighting back. We made up but not in the good make-up-sex way, and shortly after the party Jaime and Michelle invited us to a dinner/dance-type thing at their country club. Jaime and Michelle, having gone to private high school together, were high school sweethearts. Their families belonged to the same "club" in Pittsburgh. Jaime's father was a physician, and Michelle's owned a construction company.

Marcia and I went. We met them at the club and the harp and the little cartoon blue birds appeared again as soon as Jaime and Marcia saw each other. Jaime was obviously in his element. His suit was finely tailored to show off his athleticism and everyone there knew the high school star who was now playing for Pitt. Despite wearing a sport coat from my freshman year that seemed to be made to simultaneously offend one's color sense and compress my back, chest, and arm muscles, I was somewhat the hit as well.

For those who knew Pitt football, I was the bigger deal. I became a starter at defensive end two games into my freshman season and, this being near the spring of our sophomore year, I was a solid two-year starter. Jaime, although being local and the same class as me, had never started or even played in a game yet. For those who knew Pitt football, Michelle's dad being one of those, I was the real deal. Almost as soon as we got there, Michelle's father pulled me to the bar and the good ole boys' club gathered there bought me many drinks.

I shook a lot of hands and got patted on the back and encouraged to stand at the bar, tell football stories, and drink a lot of strong mixed drinks while Marcia, Jaime, and Michelle were off somewhere.

Overserved is what I believe they call it. Judging by the drunken roars of wealthy male Pitt football fans at the bar with me, it was a funny and impressive feat when, while demonstrating a move I used against West Virginia, the stitching in the back of my coat ripped completely open. Fueled by this appreciation of what results from combining cheap tailoring, rapid movement, overdeveloped musculature and consumption of dark alcohol served in a fine, smooth glass with clinking ice cubes, I took it upon myself to free my arms. While the hearty laughs continued, I slurredly stated, "This damn jacket was made for a wide reliever" and flexed every muscle I had. I did one of those Arnold Schwarzenegger double-fisted, hands up near the face bicep flexes and, true to the lack of fine workmanship, the sleeves tore apart at the front bicep area. This immediately caused another roar—nothing like drunken country club guys thinking something is hilarious—and then some Dean Martin–looking dude yelled, "Hey, Dean, not only is that thing made for a wide *reliever*, haha, but those colors are straight from a Peter Max painting. Hahaha!" I didn't know what a Peter Max painting was, so I thought it was time to leave this group of harrumphing drunken socialites.

At a dark corner table, I found Jamie, Marcia, and Michelle. The three of them were giggling about something. I stood at the side of the table in my Incredible Hulk jacket. When Marcia looked up, she nearly screamed.

"What happened, Dean? Did someone beat you up, what happened?"

"I think we should go."

"I'm not ready to go just yet."

I didn't feel like arguing, explaining, convincing, or whatever other "-ing" there was, when Jaime came to my rescue.

"I, er . . . we can take Marcia home, Dean."

I just said all right and left. Fortunately, it was big enough and dark enough in the club that I made my way out without having to wave a farewell to the laughing gang at the bar.

I drove home, not remembering much about the drive, but the next morning Marcia called, waking me to tell me she thought we should take a break. After that, we rarely saw each other on campus until she left.

Michelle and I ended up in each other's arms and in each other's beds shortly after Jaime and Marcia did the same. It seemed only natural. Michelle really was very pretty, and she was easy to fall back on. After all, my primary focus was football. Her construction-company–owning dad, John, loved me. We were both big, glad-handing drinking guys. He knew I had a shot at pro ball. In fact, I sometimes think that since he knew the Rooneys, who owned the Pittsburgh Steelers, so well, and at the time I was so serious with Michelle, he persuaded them to draft me with their last pick, in the last round of the NFL draft. Even if so, they got their money's worth in four solid years of defensive end play from me.

Michelle and I got married in late July, right before my rookie training camp, and divorced shortly after the Steelers released me almost five years later. Maybe things would have been different with Marcia, maybe I wouldn't have drunk my way out of pro football and into a police department. Maybe we'd be married with children somewhere. Oh well, I generally tried not to live in the past and all this history revision had consumed my beach-walking time and led me back into the Greta Garbo hotel hallway and up to the door of my room.

With my French doors open and the last remaining laughter from children splashing in the pool wafting in from the balcony, I fell asleep on the couch while watching a guy called the Dog Whisperer tame crazy dogs. He did it primarily by loudly whispering something like "sshhtt" to the dog. I supposed it caused the dog to think "what the hell?" and then forget it was pissed about something. My mind caught up in the show, the last thing I remember before falling asleep was hearing "sshhtt."

CHAPTER EIGHT

I woke up a couple hours later, turned off the television, got ready for bed, and slept soundly under the cool sheets. Of course, I woke up at an ungodly early hour and went for a long jog on the beach. It occurred to me during my run that Joey, the bellman, bellboy, whatever he was, may be the man, boy, whatever, to help me find out where Marcia and Jaime's place was.

After showering and eating oatmeal with honey, bananas, and walnuts and drinking coffee and orange juice at my tiki hut place, I set out on my Joey hunt. I walked by the front desk, saying good morning to the Hispanic beauty, and toward the front door. I saw Joey struggling with getting some suitcases out of the trunk of a large Cadillac that apparently belonged to an older couple. He placed the suitcases on a roller cart thing. I wondered if that thing had a name. He wheeled it in through the front doors and I waited as he wheeled it beside the front desk and guided the elders to the Hispanic beauty. Immediately, Joey turned around, smiled, and came to me.

"Mr. Hunter, how are you today, sir?"

"I'm great, Joey; just call me Dean."

"Cool, Dean."

"Joey, I was wondering if you could find out where someone lives, over at the Lago Mar Condos?"

"Well, if they live at the Lago Mar Condos, don't they live at the Lago Mar Condos?"

"Yes, yes, I mean, can you find out what unit? These are old friends of mine, and I just need to know where to go to surprise them."

"Sure, Dean, what are their names?"

"Jaime and Marcia."

"Oh ho, nice . . . these two girls live there alone?"

"No, no, it's a boy and a girl, no, I mean a guy and a girl, well, a man and a woman . . . they're my age."

"Oh," he said with very apparent disappointment.

"Devine and Hutchinson . . . Jaime Devine and Marcia Hutchinson," I added with some urgency. As if focusing on giving him the last names in a somewhat urgent and forceful manner would improve his chance of success.

"Joey," the Hispanic beauty whispered nicely our way.

Joey said, "I'll be able to find out a little later; where'll you be?"

"At the pool—thanks, Joey."

"No problem," and he turned and went to help the old people. I headed up to my room to change and head out to the pool to relax all day.

I went out to the pool and, despite the early hour, it was filling up with families. I found a lounge chair in what I thought might be a secluded area and decided to sit down, well sort of lie down, on my back. Given the seventies vibe of the place, I expected big silver metal ashtrays on stands beside the chairs. I lay down and closed my eyes. I must have been tired because the next thing I knew I was waking up to hear the heavy breathing of a man rearranging his chair very near me. I opened my eyes and saw a heavyset, ruddy-looking man with a lot of yellow-looking hair and a woman who was less descriptive with him. The man sat with his lounge chair right beside me and said "howdy." I said "hi," not too enthusiastically. Twenty minutes later, after "Larry" continued to make comments directed toward me, I gave up trying to nap and turned my attention to him and "Sally." He wanted to know my name, so I told him Dean Hunter. Larry was thinking. Larry and Sally were from Cleveland. God, was everyone in Florida from Cleveland?

"Hey, wait, I know you—you used to play for the Steelers, right?"

I said yes, a long time ago.

"Haha, man your name just come up the other day, back in Cleveland, I can't believe this. Dean 'Big Game' Hunter. My friends and I were talkin' football and we remembered that play you made in Cleveland. Haha Sally, this guy was a good player for the Steelers but this one time, hahaha… a pass gets batted and Dean here, he grabs it out of the air, an interception you know… well, he gets turned around and runs the wrong way, haha, actually broke tackles and everything but ends up in the wrong endzone for a safety. Haha. That was crazy, Dean."

"Yeah," I said. Jesus. Having to relive a play that I saw too often in football folly clips. But it was a hell of a run, even if the last tackle I broke was from my own player trying to stop me. Just then Joey came over and motioned for me to come over by the trash can where he was standing.

"Sorry to take you away from your friends, Dean, but I found out where your other friends live."

"Oh yeah, in those condos?" as I motioned toward the low-lying white building.

"Yes, they are unit 2B, second floor. Two bedroom, nice place with an ocean view. Not cheap to buy."

"OK, great, thanks, Joey." I handed him a twenty.

Joey headed back to the shade of the lobby, I turned and said to obnoxious Larry and his wife, "Hey, Larry and Sally, nice to meet you but something came up and I have to go. Take care."

Larry struggled to get his fat lips off the straw of his fruity drink and yelled too loudly, "See ya, Big Game, haha!"

I didn't think there was any point in waiting so I slipped my shirt on and, in my bathing suit, I went right over to the condos. I walked past the pool and found a stairway off to the left. It was sort of an open air affair of a stairway, cement steps with spaces in between and a metal railing. I got to the second floor and was able to locate 2B very easily. I went to the door and knocked. I didn't care if Jaime answered. I didn't know what I would say if he did, but I didn't care. I didn't even care if Marcia answered and I really didn't know what I would say to her. All this not caring who answered and not knowing what to say didn't seem to matter anyway as no one was answering. I knocked several more times, at varying degrees of loudness, but nothing. As I started to leave, I haphazardly reached out and turned the handle and the door opened. I hesitated. I had learned something being a cop all those years and one of those somethings was to trust your instincts. This didn't feel right. The door was only open a few inches but I could tell it was very dark inside, a sleeping a hangover off in the middle of a beautiful day sort of dark.

I carefully inched the door open. This wasn't the inner city but I thought how I'd feel much better if I had my police handgun with me. But the new vegetarian, reggae-listening, nonalcoholic me was, unfortunately, a gun free me as well. In actuality, because of the inner darkness and quiet, I was more afraid of the non-moving I might find than anyone that might be moving. As I stepped in, I didn't notice anything unusual. Thankfully, there was not that smell. There was no unusual smell at all, which was a major relief. Everything was quiet and dark and the temperature was cool. So I stepped in. I didn't turn on the light, I just stepped in and left the door open a little so I could see my way around. I could see that I was in a big main room that ended on the far wall in what appeared to be a wall of windows that was completely blocked off by closed vertical blinds. It was very cool. The air conditioning must have been set low. A dark cool. I stood for a second, with the only sound being the very distant sounds of the pool activity of the hotel at the Lago Mar. I took a few more steps, quietly. I was convinced there was no one in 2B with me, until the light suddenly went on, and at the door I had just come through appeared three men. Two so very large and one not so very large. The two so very large were almost twin-like in their squareness. I had a feeling they would not be the ones talking to me, and I was right. The shorter, out-of-shape one—who I was assuming was the "brains" of the operation—said,"Who do we have here? Mr. Robin Condos? What the fuck are you doin' here, man?"

I responded, "Fine, thank you."

"No, dumbfuck, what the fuck are you doin' here?" His "fucks" had a Hispanic undertone to them; he appeared to be about three-fourths Hispanic. Familiar. He looked very familiar to me.

"Huh, fucknose?"

"Fucknose?" I said in a truly quizzical manner, because I had never heard the word "fucknose."

"I never heard the word 'fucknose,'" I said

"Me either," said the block of the man to his left.

The smaller guy snapped, "Shut the fuck up!" and turned back to me. "Yes 'fucknose,' what the fuck are chew doin' here?"

"The door was open so I thought I'd come in and say hello."

"Oh, is that right?" He looked side to side at each of the blocks of men while smiling.

Before he looked back at me, I said, "What the fuck are you doin' here, fuckhead?" It still bothered me that we had left off with him calling me "fucknose."

He turned serious and I swear his talking got more Hispanic. "Listen, jew should know that we are serious mens and have been watchin' this place and are very suspicious of some gringo drivin' a hippie mobile breakin' into our good friends' apartment. Sorry for you but it's time for us to make a citizen's arrest. No, Mr. Fucknose, since you are not cooperating, it is time for us to commit an act of police brutality."

He looked again at each blockman.

It's funny what things go through your mind right before you think you are going to get in a fight. As they were stepping to me, I remember thinking, *Goddamn it, why am I wearing sandals?*

The blockman who like me had never heard the word "fucknose" came at me a little ahead of the other blockman.

They didn't come fast, more like sumo wrestlers. I didn't know, if I just stood there offering no resistance, would they eventually get to me and awkwardly just wrestle me quietly and slowly to the ground? I didn't take the chance, as I threw a straight right as soon as the first blockman was within distance and, even though he tried to duck, I landed it almost squarely in the middle of his face. It hurt my hand so I knew it had hurt his face, and the word "fucknose" would probably now apply. Unfortunately, the big overhead right had resulted in exposing my right side to the other blockman and that blockman knew where to throw the punch because when he hit me in the midsection it felt like he had used a baseball bat. I went down and couldn't breathe at all. I couldn't even make a sound. I wasn't sure if I was gasping for air but I was trying. This didn't satisfy them as they each hit me several more times in the body. Blood from blockman number one's nose dripped on me as the blockmen stood over me, while the smaller guy walked up. I had a sudden empathy for fish that were caught and gasping for air.

I could barely hear the smaller man when he said, "Don't fuck with us, motherfucker, I don' know what chew are lookin' for but we've searched everywhere more than once and there's no money, no Jaime and no beetch Marcia. So, hit the road hippy fucknose motherfucker. If we see you here again, we will kill you."

I managed to grunt and the smaller guy said, "Stretch this fucker out so I can kick him."

Blockman one and blockman two grabbed either end of me and pulled me from my fetal position. I was on my back as blockman one was standing over me bleeding on my chest. I heard the smaller man say, "The ball is down, the kick is. . . ."

I looked over to see him taking a few steps toward me to kick me in the ribs. I braced for it and he kicked me. Upon impact I instinctively grunted but there was no pain. He had kicked me but I barely felt it.

" . . . good."

Blockman two yelled at the smaller man, "Man, Rafael, you can't kick a dude soccer style." Blockman two kicked me again, which really hurt, and they all three left, slamming the door on the way out.

CHAPTER NINE

lay on the cool tile floor of the condo. Between gasping and trying to groan in pain, I was thinking I knew the little guy.

As I was lying there, it came to me. Rafael . . . soccer-style kicking. The overly Hispanic guy was Ralph Herrera. Jesus, Ralph Herrera, now apparently Rafael Herrera, was a soccer-style field goal kicker at Pitt for about one year while I was there. God, I could barely think of this because of the pain to my entire midsection, but I did remember that Jaime and Herrera were really good friends and that Herrera was a kid from Florida. I didn't remember where exactly but I did remember him being a fellow Floridian at Pitt. I tried to get up but thought it best to just stay put awhile. That bastard Herrera!

I could barely roll around while I made sounds of pain that I somehow thought would get me sympathy. I don't know who would have given me sympathy but making the groans of pain seemed to me to be making some form of protest at my condition or maybe providing some kind of relief. It seemed like I was exaggerating my pain sounds for some reason. I managed to get up to one knee and look around. My ribs hurt but my breathing seemed to be getting back to normal, so that, I assumed, was a good sign. I finally stood and tried to straighten to full height. I was a little offset by the fact that I only had one sandal on. I looked around. It was a bit of a relief to see that my other sandal was on a long narrow table full of framed pictures against a wall, and not on the floor. It meant I didn't have to lean down. I limped, half crouched, and noticed that the place was in shambles. I went to get my sandal; it was propped up against a picture of Jaime on a beach in front of an open-fronted bar. Although the bar didn't seem familiar, the general feel of the scenery did. I turned the picture around; there was nothing on the back. The familiarity of the scenery was intriguing to me. I was able to slide the picture out of the little frame and I saw written in cursive on the back "Cabarete." I knew instantly that this was in the Dominican Republic. Cabarete was an area of the DR. Maurice, I, and a couple of other players had gone there once for a break. Man, I couldn't remember when but I remembered going. The only time I had been to the Dominican. I was certain Jaime had not gone with us but he was there, at the beach at Cabarete, at some time in his young life. There were other beach pictures of Jaime, in different years, different ages and shapes. But there didn't appear to be any of him and Marcia at the beach. Just him.

I looked at the other pictures, a progression of him and Marcia, together, alone, young, older, in shape, Jaime out of shape, on various beaches, standing beside small planes. A lot of pictures of Jaime by small planes. He must be into flying. I looked around some more, pulling myself away from the pictures. After slipping on the other sandal, I got rid of the limp but the crouch was still there and my ribs on both sides hurt with each little movement.

The rest of the unit was totally ransacked. All the clothes were out of the drawers, everything was overturned. Ralph or Rafael had said something about no money, no Jaime or no Marcia being there. So, I began to think that Jaime and Marcia must have left with a lot of money but then I knew that Marcia did not know where Jaime was. At least last time I talked to her she didn't. So maybe Jaime and a lot of money were missing from Rafael and the two blockmen. Anyway, all this thinking was starting to give me a headache that I didn't need to go along with the ache in my ribs. I thought there was nothing in this unit that I could look for since I didn't even know *what* I was looking for.

I crouched my way out of the unit and onto the balcony. It was incredibly hot and sunny, and maneuvering down the steps to the ground floor was really difficult. I would alternate sides to hold on to the banister to even out the pain to the ribs. Even the front of my stomach was hurting.

I crouch-walked my way back to the hotel area without anyone noticing my bizarre style of walking and the blood on the front of my shirt. I wasn't bleeding; it was blockman one's blood, but there seemed to be a lot on me. I got to my floor and got to my room without anyone noticing, for which I was relieved. I was able to pull my shirt off and make my way to the couch. It was only a matter of minutes until there was knocking on my door.

"Dean!" Pound, pound, pound. "Dean!" Pound, pound, pound.

I recognized the voice of Joey.

"Yes, Joey," I said in less than a forceful voice. It hurt to talk.

"You OK?"

"Yeah, I can't come to the door but I'm fine."

"Listen, Dean, I'm opening the door myself. Here I come."

I thought it easier to not respond and let him come in. He did and stood at the door looking at me on the couch.

"Man, you OK? Everybody saw you limping around, crouched over, with blood all over you like you been shot. You OK?"

"Jesus," I managed.

Joey saw there was no blood, I told him I wasn't shot and that I had fallen down the steps and that I was OK. He got me two icepacks from the hotel and eventually left me alone. I fell asleep with the TV on to nothing in particular.

Sleep seemed to help, but when I woke, everything was dark except the TV. The ice bags had melted. One was on the floor and the other near my hip on the couch, cold and wet. The dog guy was "ssshting" at some mean dog on the

TV. I wondered if that would work on humans. On the blockmen in particular.

It was hard getting off the couch. I basically slowly rolled. The ribs on both sides, the front of my stomach and my hand all throbbed. I struggled to take my shorts off but I did, and I got into bed after turning dog guy off. The bed, sheets, and darkness felt good.

Surprisingly, I slept well. The children's pool noise coming from behind the thick curtain woke me up, which in turn reminded me of the pain. The day was pretty uneventful. I stayed in the room the entire day. There was a dog guy marathon on and I watched too many of those shows. Joey checked on me twice. I got room service twice and, in between grunts of pain, made some phone calls. Rose was doing fine. I told her I would be home soon as the blockmen had pretty much convinced me that I was here for no reason. I thought I had one thing to do tomorrow and then that would be a good day to move on.

I also called Detective John Kotagides of the Pittsburgh Police Department. John and I were old friends and working mates. John was older than me and, very early on in my police career, had taken me under his wing. He was largely responsible for my quick rise through the ranks and into the DB.

We bullshitted for a while before I informed him why I had called him. The address of one Ralph "Rafael" Herrera. I had told John that I thought he would be in Fort Lauderdale, Miami, somewhere in that area. It didn't take John long. Old "Rafael" lived in Miami. I wrote the address down, talked with John a little more, and hung up in time for a new episode of the dog guy.

The next day came quickly and the pain didn't get much better, but I was tired of lying around in my room and decided to get out.

I was up early and pretty much had my choice of where to sit by the pool. I sat out of view from where I had been with Larry and his wife. I didn't feel like being the subject of football follies for another day.

I fell asleep in the shade of the pool area only to be awakened by Joey. Joey was pulling on my big toe.

"Hey, Dean . . . Dean."

"Aw, hey Joey. . . . Oohh, aww."

"Dean there's a woman that wants to meet with you."

"Really?"

"Yes, she's in cabana number three."

"What is cabana number three?"

"See those rows of cabanas; she's in number three over there. Not bad, around your age, I would guess"

I walked sort of like John Wayne past the pool to the cabana area. It wasn't that I wanted to walk like John Wayne; I didn't even really like the way John Wayne walked. It was just that the rib pain caused me to walk like that. I'm not even sure it looked like a John Wayne walk, but it felt like it and I imagined it looked like it. Anyway I made it past cabanas one and two and arrived at the opening of three.

Inside, under a big hat and behind big sunglasses was Marcia in a lounge chair. I leaned against the pole at the entrance, sort of doubled up a little from the ribs.

"Dean, are you constipated?"

"No, why?"

"Well, the way you are standing, and I could see you through this little flap here, walking toward this cabana and you sure are walking like you are constipated."

"No, I'm working on my John Wayne impression."

"Oh, well, that makes sense, I suppose. Listen, Dean, I'm sorry about the other day. I hardly remember it."

"That's OK, neither do I . . . but what are you doing here, in this cabana?"

"When I saw you sleeping by the pool, I thought I had to see you."

God, she looked good to me.

"Well, how did you know I would be by the pool . . . sleeping?"

"I didn't. I know I shouldn't have come back here. I was shocked when I saw you. I know someone broke into our place, so I thought I would go around the back," she said as she motioned with her hand. "I was walking around the pool and all of a sudden I saw you. I didn't know what to do, so I came into this thing and asked that boy to send you here. What are you doing here?"

"Marcia. . . . " I began. "I thought you needed my help and I thought I should help you, but I don't even know why I'm thinking I should be helping you. I don't even know what you need help for, other than I know three guys ransacked your place. What does Ralph Herrera have to do with Jaime and you?"

"Ralph Herr…?" And she started to laugh. "Oh my god, I haven't heard that in forever. I guess it is Ralph. It was Ralph, wasn't it? At Pitt. Geez, Dean, I've known him for so long as Rafael that I had forgotten he used to be Ralph."

CHAPTER TEN

She explained to me that not long after she and Jaime arrived in Key West, Jaime had found a place for them to rent and he had begun taking flying lessons. For a while, it was an ideal life for them. She didn't have to work as Jaime's parents, and hers occasionally, would send enough money for them to get by very comfortably. Jaime was flying every chance he got and was very happy. Even though she was still college age, doing nothing but exploring Key West began to get old for her. She longed to be back in school but Jaime was so happy that she decided to wait until he was fully licensed. Near that time, as he was getting close to getting his license, Rafael (previously known as Ralph) began showing up fairly regularly and meeting with Jaime. Nothing bad, usually just long lunches that she was never invited to. Rafael was always very nice to Marcia but she couldn't help noticing that the car he drove and the jewelry he wore were too showy and seemingly beyond his means, as he was roughly their age. She couldn't help but see a kid trying to play rich businessman.

Jaime graduated, or I guess got his license. He was proud and she was proud for him. He loved flying the planes that had the ability to land on the water, the seaplanes.

She was nervous as she prepared to spring on Jaime that she wanted to go back to school and there was nothing there for her in Key West. She was nervous for nothing because Jaime told her that he was thinking she should go back to school, that they had been in Key West long enough, and that, by the way, Rafael had a flying job for him in Miami. She could enroll at the University of Miami. They moved to a very nice apartment, not far from the ocean, and she enrolled. Her parents were thrilled she was back in school. Jaime began flying. He told her he was the pilot for Rafael's boss, whom they called "Whitey." According to Jaime, Whitey owned many car dealerships across the country and Jaime's job was to fly him wherever and whenever he wanted, in his private jet.

Jaime met a lot with Rafael, or at least he said he did. Marcia never saw Rafael. The meetings were always away from the apartment. Marcia was consumed with getting her business degree and hanging around her college friends. She would go back to Ohio, to her hometown of Chagrin Falls, on her college breaks.

Marcia did well in college, graduated, and immediately started working in Miami's largest real estate company. She told me the name but I don't remember because I was still distracted by the pain in my ribs. During her storytelling, I managed to John Wayne my way into the lounge chair beside her and Joey had brought her some sort of fruity alcohol drink and me a very cold Buckler nonalcoholic beer in the bottle.

Life went on for them with little or no talk of marriage, Jaime flying all the time and Marcia consumed in her work. They moved to an even nicer condo, in a high rise, with a spectacular ocean view. She remembers thinking, as the years went on, that Jaime was turning into an old man. He was not exercising and he was drinking too much. But she was busy with work and social events and they had enough fun, occasionally, that life was not that bad. But, as life goes, things changed. Marcia was bought out with a severance agreement when the real estate market started to collapse. Jaime continued to drink and not exercise. He became more and more nervous and, according to Marcia, was obsessed with the war in Iraq and how the situation was over there and, more recently, the situation in Afghanistan. He would spend several days at a time away from home flying for Whitey.

Then, one day less than a year ago, Jaime sat Marcia down, in the cool of their condo, and nervously told her that they needed to move. That he found a place in Fort Lauderdale, that he was quitting working for Whitey, and since she couldn't find work in Miami, that a change of scenery would be better for them. That they could get to know each other again, that things would be like the Key West days. She wanted to hear that.

She had asked him how he bought the Lago Mar place, which she pointed to as we sipped on our second round of drinks, how they were affording not to work. He told her he had saved a lot from working for Whitey. She didn't push it but she noticed a new nervousness. He would spend time away from the condo without explanation. He had exchanged their cell phones for new ones, with new numbers. Then, last week, a week to this day today, he left, like he often did, but he did not return. I asked her about what she did to try to find him and she had done everything she could. Her many calls all went to Jaime's voicemail. She thought about going to the police but for some reason she decided not to. She came to see me because she had remembered hearing that I was in Amelia Island. She had nowhere to turn and was frustrated being in the condo trying to find him. After visiting me, she came back to the condo to discover it trashed. She did not notice anything missing so, for some reason she really could not explain, she decided not to call the police. She always suspected Jaime was doing something with Rafael that wasn't 100 percent proper. She got out of there, thinking no one had seen her. She went to Miami and spent the night with a girlfriend of hers, but today she had decided that she could not live like this and had to go back to the condo and wait for Jaime.

I told her my part of the story. We sat in silence for a little, in the cool of the shade of cabana three, drinking our drinks, listening to the kids jumping and splashing.

Finally, she said that she couldn't believe that I had been beaten up, that their place had been torn apart or imagine that Rafael would want to hurt Jaime; maybe they were just looking for something he had. I told her that I didn't know if they wanted to hurt Jaime but that they were definitely looking for something, that the something was probably money, and that their looking had caused Jaime to leave her without explanation.

She was hungry and so was I. I asked her to have lunch with me. We ate in the seventies-carpeted restaurant with the glass windows looking out onto the pool. The restaurant was quiet; we could see the kids jumping in and out of the pool, not an adult worry at all for them. We couldn't hear their joyful laughing and yelling because of the thick glass windows. Inside the restaurant were two other tables of adults, not joyfully laughing and yelling. Marcia had an iced tea, with no alcohol, and the shrimp salad. I had salmon on toasted whole wheat bread and a water. I tried to learn as much about Jaime's actions as I could; it must have been my detective instincts kicking in because I genuinely wanted to know and couldn't help thinking that things did not look good for Jaime. I thought it may not be too late. Rafael and the blockmen obviously hadn't located Jaime and/or what they were looking for, as of yesterday, if you believed Rafael's statements to me. There was no reason to not believe them unless you believed Rafael was going to some extremes to convince me that they were still looking when in fact they weren't. Which didn't make sense. So I thought Jaime was still OK but hiding and, of course, I assured Marcia I would find him.

We finished our meal and headed up to my room. I had offered to her, with not purely carnal intentions, that she could stay with me until we figured out how safe her return to her condo would be. Of course, there were carnal intentions involved, but I also did want to help Marcia as much as I could. We passed a winking Joey as we headed to my suite. When we got there, she looked around the room and I looked at her from the door. I couldn't help but think how things would have been so different if we had stayed together. It was crazy to think that neither of us had had children. I felt that had we been together we would have started a family. She was the woman I always imagined having a family with. Not with Michelle, who was too busy being the in-shape beautiful socialite with a handsome pro football player husband for us to even think about children. The girls and women that followed all just seemed like a passing of time since then, and the older you get, the quicker that passing of time goes. So, since I was not exceptionally wealthy or a famous actor, I didn't picture myself settling down with a woman half my age and starting a family. I guess, for whatever reason, I was meant to go through life without having a child.

She was out on the balcony, and the combination of ocean breeze and low-set air conditioning, of the bright active day beyond the curtains and low-lit calm of the room, produced a highly sexual setting. Sex at a time of day that was not usual, under the right circumstances, in my opinion was not a bad thing. She turned and saw me looking at her. I snapped out of it and told her she was welcome to do anything she wanted. As I watched her go to the bedroom part of the suite. I explained to her that I had to change as I had somewhere to go. She sat on the couch as I changed into my jeans, a Bob Marley t-shirt, and my running shoes. As I came out of the bedroom area, Marcia said, "You look really good, Dean. You have really aged well."

"Thanks, you do, too, Marcia." I felt as if I had said it too seriously, too somberly. So I changed gears, "Well, the

TV is right here . . . there seems to always be a dog training guy show on that is pretty good."

She laughed, smiled, and said, "Be careful, Dean," as though she knew what I was going to do.

CHAPTER ELEVEN

After getting my keys and enduring "Geez, Dean, that was fast" from Joey, I was in the Thing speeding down 95 with the top down and Burning Spears blasting on the stereo. I found the allotment easily. I got through the security gate by saying I had an appointment at the clubhouse with Mr. Herrera. The gate went down behind me, and I drove the posted 15 miles an hour through the palm-tree-lined golf course with fountains. This was no low-rent district. In fact, it was probably a no-rent district as I am sure the association here had very strict guidelines.

Ralph, Rafael, whatever, had a nice place. It wasn't the best place in the allotment, in the best part of the allotment, but it was an impressive one story, Spanish-looking place with some elevation, sort of on a small hill. He had a short stone coral-type wall and gate around his property. I couldn't help but ask myself why you would need a gate within a gated community—did you really need to keep the other gated riffraff from entering onto your land?

I couldn't—and didn't want to—park in Ralph's driveway so I drove past and around a couple streets before making another pass. I noticed a pool service truck parked against the curb two properties down, so I pulled behind the truck and parked. Hopefully, anyone who might have a problem with me being there would think the Thing was one of the pool service worker's cars.

I walked quickly to Ralph's property and, after a very brief look around, jumped over his wall. My ribs still hurt but I was past the John Wayne stage. The good thing about these communities is that no one is ever out, so I felt pretty confident no one noticed my trespass. All was quiet on my brisk walk up the yard toward the house. There was a big shiny black Escalade in the driveway. I walked past, hoping there was no one in it as the windows were so dark there could have been four guys in there without me even knowing it. I went straight past it and into the garage. The two-car garage door was open. There was another single garage door that was not open. I went right to the several steps that led up to the door that I assumed went into the house. After slowly and quietly opening the door, I found that I was right. I was in the house; I was in a long dark hallway. There was no noise. I quietly walked down the hallway. I could see a kitchen area ahead of me and still heard no noise. I got to the end of the hall and paused, hearing nothing. The kitchen was in front of me and appeared to go to the right and left of me. I peered around the corner to the left, as I figured the majority of the house had to go in that direction. I was right: The kitchen extended a little and beyond that was a very large sunken great room and off to the right of that room were sliding doors that led out to the pool area. I heard the distant thump of bass from music out in the pool area.

I walked into the kitchen and to the right. The place was spotless, bright and airy, uncluttered, with marble countertops. I was impressed. I was making my way around the huge kitchen island as quietly as possible. I wanted to get to the window at the other wall as I thought that looked out onto the pool. It did. Much to my disappointment, when I leaned over the counter to look out the window I saw one of the blockmen sitting in the shade of a cabana area by the pool in a Tommy Bahama buttoned short-sleeve shirt and shorts. He was slightly bopping his big block head to the music and texting on his phone.

As I turned from the window to head to the great room, the silence exploded. A monster pit bull-type dog insanely started barking at me from about ten feet away. I thought I was having a heart attack. I didn't move, tried to think for a moment as the barking and slobbering and gnarling continued. Then I stood straight, took a deep breath, looked the beast in his dark, lifeless eyes, and said "sssht" as loud as I could. I thought the dog stopped for a second before it charged me head on. I broke to my left and it came with me. It bit at my leg but ended up just getting the leg of my pants. I think its tooth or teeth got caught in the jean material because as I was freaking out trying to get away I seemed to be pulling the dog with my leg as it was tearing at my jeans. I noticed a door. Opened it, did a full swing leg kick, and the dog, still attached to my jeans, went flying through the door I had just opened. I didn't know where the door led to when I had opened it but I didn't care. The dog went flying off my jeans, in the air, and through the door, which I could now see was a deep closet. The dog slammed against the back wall of the closet and I heard a yelp as I slammed the door shut. I stood still, listening, in my torn jeans, but nothing had changed.

The bassy background music still beat. It is such a weird feeling to be involved in an intense, chaotic, crazy situation, have it end abruptly and then just silence. After I got my heart rate back to normal, I started to laugh to myself as I wished that I had a video of what had just happened. But I got serious and went back to the window and saw blockman doing exactly the same thing he had been doing, bopping and texting. I tiptoed to the sliding door that led out to the pool. It was closed, as the house was air conditioned. I was able to reach the lock and lock the door without blockman noticing.

I listened intently. I heard some high-pitched singing coming from down a hallway. I went toward it.

The high-pitched singing got louder as I approached a door on the right side of the hallway. I listened: a male voice with a touch of Hispanic accent, badly off tune, singing that annoying Justin Bieber song that was on every radio you happened to hear. I didn't know the name of the song but I knew some of the words; however, I don't think the offending singer did, as I was sure he had some of the words wrong, only getting the "baby, baby, baby" part right. I listened intently against the door to try and make out any other sounds. The singing was loud and awful, but I did also hear a machine sound and the pounding of feet. I thought the offending singer to be on a treadmill, and it seemed he was to the right and back, if you went through the door. I couldn't take the singing anymore and I was certain there was no one else in that room subjecting themselves to that auditory punishment, so I decided to go in.

I quickly opened the door and briskly, almost jogging, walked to the area I suspected the singer to be. Sure enough, it was Rafael-Ralph singing and running. He freaked out as he saw me quickly approaching him. He immediately stopped singing (thank God) but was confused as to whether to grab for his headphones or turn off the treadmill. He did a little of both. When I got to him, the headphones were half off his head and he tried to stop running on the moving treadmill, obviously not thinking quickly enough that he could jump off. He was stumbling in a half-falling run, arms and legs flailing. I grabbed him by the shirt near his shoulder and yanked him off then, straight out of the Three Stooges, I grabbed the back of his shirt and pulled it completely over his head. He was bent over at the waist, saying "no, please," as I heard Bieber still singing on inside his shirt. I didn't know what to do, so I pushed him. He fell to his side with the shirt still completely over his head. He looked like a turtle as he lay on his side repeating "no, please." I lined up and kicked him in the stomach, hard. The kick hurt my ribs but probably hurt his stomach more.

"That's how you kick, Ralph. Lou Groza style, straight on."

He was gasping for air, shirt still over his head, Bieber still singing as I turned to leave. I had done what I came to do. I wasn't even thinking about Jaime. I just wanted to let Ralph know that he could not get over on me. As I turned, blockman one complete with huge white bandage on his nose was standing in the doorway with a shiny silver handgun pointed directly at me.

"'Ands up," he said in a Mike Tyson tone, and clearly unable to pronounce the word due to his nasal situation. I looked at my hands and they were already up. This was not the first time I had had a gun pointed at me.

Ralph was coming around as blockman one and I just stared at each other. Ralph's groaning was lessening and he managed to pull the shirt off from over his head, but the music could still be heard from the headphones.

"Hey, Ralph, can you turn that crap music off?" I said. Blockman one smiled. Ralph stumbled to his feet and threw the headphones in the corner. He was hunched over, holding his stomach and looking at me from the side.

"Chew call me Ralph; what's your name?"

"Bond . . . James Bond," I said.

Blockman one chuckled a little.

"No, really, chew got me very curious, I'm thinking I know you." He forgot to pronounce "you" as "chew."

"You do," I said. "Dean Hunter."

There was a moment's hesitation as he searched through the air in his head.

"Aw, yeah man," a big smile broke out on his chubby face. "I see it now . . . really, man, you haven't changed much . . . Jesus, Dean 'Big Game' Hunter right here in my house!" He looked to blockman one. "Hey, Mookie, check it, this is Big Game Hunter, helluva football player here, played in the League. . . . Man, put that gun down, we're old friends

. . . right, Dean? We're good? You aren't gonna kick me anymore, or punch Mookie in his nose?"

"No, Ralph, we're good. I just had to return the kick."

"Good, you don't know how much I had to pay for Mookie's nose," Ralph said as he pointed to "Mookie. "Plus, Mookie's a big pussy; he hates doctors, cried more about going there than your punch, man . . . and we ain't got insurance, so I had to pay the bill myself . . . but, hey, how you been, man?"

"Good, good, Ralph."

"What was chew doin' in Jaime's crib, man . . . when we saw you?"

"I was looking for Jaime; Marcia's worried."

"Beetch Marcia," he said under his breath.

"Yeah, well, she's worried about him and asked me to help find him. You know where he is?"

"Les go talk," he said.

CHAPTER TWELVE

We ended up by the pool. He had blockman two mix him a drink of some kind. Apparently one he drank often and that blockman two made often because there was virtually no communication between the two about his drink. When I was told they had no nonalcoholic beer, I settled for an iced tonic water. We sat in the shade of several large pool umbrellas. The pool and surrounding landscaping was very impressive. There were palm trees that offered big palm leaf shade. Although the house didn't front a waterway, it was very near a channel and you could see the tops of large boats quietly cruising by over the fence that enclosed Ralph's place. It had the feel of waterfront; it was nice.

As we were sitting down, "Mookie" unlocked the sliding door and slid it open. Very high-pitched and nasally, he yelled at Ralph, "Nay, nook who's here; he was in the clonset."

"Bruno . . . come on, Bruno," Ralph called to the dog.

The dog slowly, head down, made its way through the sliding door and out into the bright sunshine. He was very obviously limping.

"Oh, Bruno boy," Ralph said in that baby talk voice adults often do to their pets. "Chew hurt your leg?"

Thankfully, dogs can't talk and Bruno, despite being asked the question directly, did not respond with "Yeah Ralph, that big bozo next to you threw me in the closet." At which point I would have had to state my side of the case that he attacked me first. But, in fact, the dog didn't seem to recognize me at all. It didn't shy away or growl or anything but instead just limped over to Ralph's chair and lay beside him in the shade as I tried to not make my ripped pant leg so obvious.

"Well geez, Dean, you look great. Like you could still play and I bet gettin' the ladies still isn't a problem for you."

"Thanks, Ralph, you look great too," I lied. "Ralph, if we're gonna talk a while, you mind if I light up a cigar?"

"Hell no, brotha. In fact, I got some good-ass Cubans here. Hey, Mookie, can you get us some cigars from the inside bar? Get one for yourself," he yelled across the pool to Mookie, who was talking with blockman two. Mookie waved and headed through the sliding doors. Ralph seemed to be an OK employer, taking Mookie to the doctor, paying for it, and allowing him to have one of his good-ass Cubans.

As Ralph was telling me his story, Mookie had reappeared, gave me a cut cigar, lit it while breathing heavily through his bandage, and left us. Ralph had started on his second drink. This was actually feeling pretty good . . . comfortable chair, shade, poolside, cold drink, and fine cigar.

According to Ralph, he left Pitt before Jaime and Marcia because the coaching staff, despite intently recruiting him from the Miami area, had a thing about Hispanics. I tried to sympathize as much as possible but the truth was I barely remembered Ralph. In the hierarchy of college football, it is sometimes difficult to remember players who were below you on the depth chart and especially if they played a different position and left early. I think it was pleasing to Ralph that I called him Ralph because that meant that I remembered him as part of the Pitt team.

Anyway, Jaime had gotten a hold of him when they moved to Key West. They had been friends at Pitt and Jaime told Ralph how he wanted to be a pilot and asked Ralph if he had any contacts. Ralph was working for a guy that owned many "car dealerships" and he thought "Whitey" might need some flying duty.

"Man, my man Jaime, he loves to fly."

I was encouraged by his use of the present tense. We talked and smoked, but it was getting dark and I needed to get back. Ralph wasn't going to tell me any more than that "Jaime has a lot of Whitey's money" and that Whitey was very upset about it and that Ralph hoped he could find Jaime. All Ralph had found was Jaime's car parked at their usual club in Miami with nothing in it but Jaime's cell phone with all the contacts deleted. Ralph didn't tell me how Jaime got Whitey's money, what it was for, or what Whitey really did. He did expound on his thoughts that it was all that "Beetch" Marcia's fault. That she was money hungry and that she probably convinced Jaime to take the money. I told him that I honestly believed that she didn't know where he was or why he left. I didn't share the fact that I knew where she was now. I left off, in my story, with her leaving me in Amelia Island.

Before I left, I shook hands, the way cool guys and athletes do, with both blockmen (Mookie and Manny), each of us muscling up during the clasp and hug part of the routine. After exchanging numbers, I assured Ralph that I would let him know if I found anything out, but I also told him I was done searching. In fact, despite thinking that I should be done with all of this, I didn't think that I would be. To make Ralph feel good, I even told Mookie and Manny that Ralph had been a hell of a kicker back in the day. I even pet Bruno on my way out.

The ride back was uneventful. It was a beautiful, clear Florida night. I pulled into the Lago Mar; it was quiet out front and I parked the car myself. I walked through the expansive opening of the front entrance and toward the stairwell that led to my room. Joey stopped me.

"Dean, she's out by the pool, told me to tell you. Man, I knew you weren't gay, even with the flower car and pink keychain thing. . . . I told Lia; she didn't believe me."

"Lia?"

"Yeah, she works the front desk . . . beautiful but she got them cold eyes that can order you around."

"Jesus, she thinks I'm gay? Never mind, Marcia's out by the pool?"

"Yes, guess she didn't hold that quick performance against you, give you another chance, maybe."

"Joey, do you ever take time off from this job?"

"No, man, I can't, place would fall apart without me."

I walked out by the big pool but other than a family getting a night swim in, there was nothing there. I went through the hedge divider and approached the smaller pool by the condos. Marcia was reclined in a lounge chair near the pool. As I got closer, she noticed me and stood. I walked over to her. She was wearing a long, flowing, lightweight skirt and a short, low-cut top. Obviously, she disregarded my advice. She had left my room and been back to her condo as I certainly didn't pack that outfit with my stuff.

"Wow, you look great," I managed to get out. She came close and I instinctively took her by her arms. We kissed. It was like we had never left off, it was so natural. We had done it hundreds of times before and it seemed that time did nothing to erase it. She felt great to me.

I held her against me. She felt small and vulnerable.

"Dean, I can't. . . . I do love Jaime and I need to find him."

"I understand, Marcia." It killed me as I wanted more than anything to rekindle what I knew we had.

"Listen," I continued, "I'll find him, I promise you that." As I immediately thought, "Why? Why did I just say that?"

We stayed together, her head against my chest, for a few more minutes.

"I should be going," she said, "it's fine to stay in my place, isn't it?"

"Yes, it is. . . . I had a talk with Ralph and let him know that you really knew nothing about where Jaime might be."

"Dean, why are they trying to find him?"

"I guess he has a lot of Whitey's money."

"Oh," she said this sadly, as if realizing that, with a lot of money, it appeared that Jaime didn't need her.

After some thought she said, "I think I am going back to Ohio."

"OK, I think that's a good idea, Marcia. I'm headed back to Amelia in the morning. Are your parents still in that Christmas Card town?"

She managed a small laugh. "Yes, same house, same everything; they are doing great."

"Then I will know how to get a hold of you."

She walked over to a lounge chair and picked up her purse. As she walked away, the smell of her hair seemed to come closer. I went to her and stood close as she wrote her cell phone number down on a small pad. I took the little piece of paper, folded it, and took the notepad and pen from her and wrote down the number for my house and the bar. I slipped the pad and pen back into her purse.

We hugged again, and as we let go our hands joined. Her hand feeling small in mine, not a young girl's hands anymore.

I slowly released her and turned to walk away.

"Dean, you will find Jaime, won't you?"

"Yes, I will, I promise." I knew I would. For some reason, I knew I would.

CHAPTER THIRTEEN

I didn't sleep much that night. I tried the TV but that didn't help. I no longer believed in the dog guy since I discovered my leg fling worked a lot better than his "sshhtt."

So I watched the sun rise from my balcony with coffee and a cigar. It was quiet and fresh with the distant sounds of the waves. This was the only time I had been here that I didn't hear the sound of children somewhere. But with the approaching sun, came activity. First, pool preparation workers in their white shirts, then mothers placing towels on lounge chairs to reserve their family's spots near the pool. I thought it time to leave, and I packed up.

When I walked out through the lobby area, I didn't see Joey anywhere. I approached the very pretty Lia at the desk and, in my most manly voice, asked her where Joey was. She told me that Joey was not due in until the afternoon. I told her tell him goodbye for me, gave her a fifty-dollar bill to give to him and, as I was writing down the Sandy Turtle's name, address, and phone number, told her to tell him to stop by sometime. She thanked me and I gave her a twenty just because she was so pretty and nice.

In the Thing, I drove slowly by Marcia and Jaime's condo, kind of hoping Marcia might be up and about. I didn't see her, so I lit up my second cigar of the day and headed over the bridge, crossing the intercoastal in the delicate warmth of the morning sun.

Being a creature of habit. I drove until I got to St. Augustine, listening to Bob, Third World, and other oldies, but I also tried out some new stuff by Stacious, Tarrus Riley, and Mavado. The Turtle was becoming locally known for a place to hear great old and new reggae tunes. Just because I was aging, I didn't want to lose touch with what was new.

I was more than starving when I pulled in St. Augustine. My solution was to present myself at the Present Moment Café and devour guacamole and salsa, followed by the

Sunlight Burger with caramelized onions and a dark O'Doul's.

A black Onyx was my cigar of choice for cigar number three of the day as I headed back up the highway to Fernandina.

I was crossing the bridge onto Amelia Island at around 5:00 p.m. Amelia Island has a distinct smell to it that some newcomers hate. It dates back to the paper mill factory of my childhood. To me, it's home and, with the exposed top of the Thing, Omega blasting and the afternoon beginning its fade away, it felt good to be home. I took in a deep breath as I sped over the bridge. I took a right near the bottom of the bridge to take the longer way to the Turtle. I drove under the canopy of trees that grew over the road leading past Summer Beach and the Ritz. The road is always shady and there are cricket sounds even during the middle of the day. I passed the entrance and the tee box of the Ritz golf course and turned right onto Fletcher.

The early evening was breezy and fresh. I was anxious to get to my little bar. I pulled up and there was a black Mercedes with tinted windows parked in my El Jefe spot. I suspected I knew whose it was, and I smiled to myself.

Yep, I entered the bar and no one noticed, because the entire place was gathered around Maurice. Maurice Woods, former Heisman Trophy Finalist, former number two overall NFL draft pick, three-time Pro Bowler, and now star of the silver screen was holding court in the bar of which he was half-owner. When he saw me, he was getting his picture taken with a young woman I didn't know; he winked and when the picture was over he thanked her and made his way to me. We soulfully clasped hands and hugged long and hard. We were like brothers; he was my best friend and, no matter how long it had been since we last saw each other, we still felt the same.

"OK, gay boys, you can stop with your huggin' and shit," Rose yelled from behind the bar over the reggae that was thumping.

After Maurice signed a couple more autographs, I noticed that the bar crowd seemed larger than usual. Maurice got a cognac from Rose, I got a Bucklers, and we went out on the front porch and each lit up a mild Macanudo Hampton Court I provided. We sat for a while not really saying anything.

Apparently, Maurice was in Savannah, Georgia, getting ready to begin shooting another *GI Joe* film. He was in top physical condition. The breeze from the ocean was nice, some shrimp boats were cruising by, the rocking chairs were big and cool from the shade. At this very moment, life was good, and Maurice and I knew and appreciated it. We no longer talked about our dreams like we did when we were kids sitting together under the shade of the tree outside J & G's store drinking our artificially flavored slushies. Now we didn't say anything, just sat enjoying the quiet time together.

Jerry came bounding up the steps. "Well, look at these two studs. . . . Jesus, you both look like you could go out and suit up."

"Don't think so, Jerry, I know I'd at least pull a hamstring and I never ran fast enough to pull a hamstring," I responded.

"Maurice, man, how you been? I see you all over the entertainment news; you're getting really famous."

"Haha," Maurice smiled his trademark cool smile and nodded his head slowly.

"Where's that cutie, Sara—she working now?" Jerry had lost his Maurice focus and was on a mission to harass Sara.

"Yes, she's working, and she is a cutie, Jerry, but she's very young."

"Dean, I couldn't partially agree with you more. Nice seein' you, Maurice, keep up the good work. I'll get your number from Dean and give you a call when I'm in Hollywood." He said this loudly, for everyone to hear, as he headed through the door.

"Man, you give that dude my number and we're done," Maurice laughed.

We were quiet again until I decided to tell him about Marcia and Jaime. Maurice listened, only asking how Marcia looked and whether or not we did anything. I told him about the kiss and that conversation. I felt like a ninth grade school girl talking about a kiss from a guy I was after. He remembered Ralph.

"Listen, Dean, you should just stay away from this one. I know you want Marcia to come back to you but she made it clear. You're second team. You don't know if Jaime's gonna show up dead somewhere or what. Although, it seems like any dude that hires Ralph to be one of his main men might not be such a tough guy."

"True," I said. "You may be right, but it seems there's a lot of money involved. Then again, I can't imagine that Ralph would've hurt or killed Jaime if he'd have found him in the condo instead of me."

"Maybe Ralph didn't know they were gonna hurt or kill him. Maybe Ralph finds him and those two tough guys do it without Ralph suspecting they were going to."

"I don't know, man; I don't know what I'm gonna do."

"I know, and I'm tellin' you, don't get involved."

"Whatever. . . ."

"I know . . . whatever happens, happens; same laid-back attitude you always had," he said, softly laughing. "Man, people called me laid back and I tell them they ain't seen shit till they see my man, Dean."

"Whatever."

"Haha . . . whatever," and he took a drink of his cognac and a puff of his Macanudo.

We finished our cigars, talked about the bar, some of the women in his life, his son, and then he left. He was driving back to Savannah, as he had the initial cast meeting tomorrow and, despite me telling him many times to spend the night at my place, he wanted to get to the hotel there. He gave me his contact information there and told me again to forget about Marcia and Jaime. I told him again "whatever. . . ."

I left the Turtle at about 11:00. Rose said she'd close up and there were only a couple people left. I hadn't seen Beans at the Turtle and hadn't gone by his place, so I still had the Thing. I drove straight down Atlantic Avenue, turned left on my street, and pulled in front of my house. Lori was sitting on the front porch. I turned the music down and eased into my little driveway. As I walked up to the porch, the warm breeze pushed her perfume to me. She didn't say anything and neither did I until I was on the porch.

"Hey," I said, soft and low.

"Dean, I'm sorry," she said in her southern twang. "I talked to Rosie and I know now, I shouldn't a dumped that drink in your lap."

"Oh well, let's go inside."

After I showered, we more than made up for our misunderstanding, and I slept very soundly. Lori spent the night.

CHAPTER FOURTEEN

I was up early the next morning, exchanged the Thing for my car, and was hugging the curve on Fletcher with the warm early morning wind blowing my hair and the ashes of my Onyx all over the place. My Corvette, like my clothes, had more than a few burn holes. Oh well, the hazards of enjoyment.

When I got to the Turtle, nothing had changed and I partook in my routine. The coffee, the Onyx, the ocean breeze mixed with the sounds of the waves and seagulls were a perfect blend.

As I sat in Marcia's chair, the morning sun was warming my face and body. I was almost in a meditative state induced by the waves softly crashing, the seagulls, and the sun. But my thoughts of Marcia continued. Where was she now? If I let this thing with Jaime just die down, would she forget about him and could we start over? I painfully realized that if she never heard from Jaime again, she would never forget about him. I also knew Maurice was right and that I would not let it go. I convinced myself that if I found Jaime, I could reveal him for what he was and Marcia would be done with him. My thoughts were that Jaime had committed some serious wrong that had caused him great paranoia and caused him to flee. Maybe I could expose it to Marcia. I knew that rooting for the starter to get injured so that I could get my playing time wasn't the best way to approach it, but it's all I had.

I heard someone coming slowly, walking around the porch from the side of our place where my car was parked. It was Laura. Laura Barnett was always on a mission. She struggled, in her flowing hippy gowns, to sort of stomp her way up the steps to the porch where I sat. I just watched her. We didn't say a thing to one another until she sat in a rocking chair across the porch from me.

Finally, she said, "Good morning, Dean."

"It is, Laura, how have you been?" I asked her.

Unlike Beans's wife, who just recently discovered it was cool to be environmentally friendly, Laura was the real deal. She had long, thick, sort of bundled graying hair and wore no makeup. Her love of nature didn't translate to a love of physical fitness. She was not in terrible shape, but she wasn't in great or maybe even good shape. I thought I knew that she did yoga but I had never really seen her do any form of exercise. I couldn't picture it. She gave off a wise, intelligent vibe, sort of how you picture Indian chiefs. Her skin was brown, not too wrinkly.

"I'm worried," She was always worried and I knew about what.

"Laura, nothing's changing; there are no new developments being built."

I didn't know this. Well, I knew there was nothing new being built, but I didn't know that there was nothing in the planning stages. I stopped reading newspapers when I was a detective. I know, not very detective-like to not read newspapers; I don't know how many times I heard "didn't you see it in the paper?" I just learned that most reporters had a slant, an opinion, a built-in bias that shaped their reporting. I had been in enough actual situations that I read about later and didn't recognize the situation being reported as the same as I had been in. Therefore, I stopped reading. I figured if this is how my situations were being reported, then I could not trust the reporting of situations of which I did not have personal knowledge. At any rate, I took a guess with Laura about "nothing's changing." Odds are, I would have heard if something was changing.

"I know," she wearily replied, "but that's when things always seem to be the most dangerous."

We left it there for the moment. I was waiting for her to ask. She always asked. I sometimes thought she had a calendar at home and had me scheduled to be asked every couple of weeks.

"Would you like a cup of coffee?" I asked.

"Why, yes Dean, that would be very nice."

I knew she took it black. We had done this before. I went inside, the lightweight screened door slamming behind me, making a sound bigger than it was, the fans slowly spinning, and the place enveloping me in its cool shade. I poured coffee into her BeachSaver mug that I kept. She had given it to me when I signed her petition and donated money to her beach and wave saving foundation.

It was always nice to see her warm smile when I would hand her the coffee in this mug and, like so many times before, it was there again when she raised her eyes to me as I rejoined her on the porch.

"You haven't been approached, have you?" she finally asked.

"No, Laura, I haven't, and if I was, you would be the first know."

"I know Dean, just have to keep up . . . you don't know how sneaky they can be."

"They" were developers. Laura was losing her fight to save American Beach and she was worried about the rest of the coastline. Her moment in the sun had come when she and her organization, the First Coast Chapter of the BeachSaver Foundation, had forced the Ritz Carlton, down the beach, to build farther away from the ocean than their original plans.

During that time, she finally had a soapbox for her efforts to ". . . discourage development in vulnerable areas and support efforts to build structures farther landward of eroding shorelines." She even got some national attention. Laura gained a lot of credibility then because, in most people's opinions, she didn't oppose the development that included the Ritz in its entirety but just the initial plans of building it so very close to the shoreline. In the end, the Ritz built a building that had beautiful grounds and was as environmentally friendly as one could expect and that supplied my little place with bored younger patrons.

It was her Super Bowl and she won and, like Joe Namath, she would enjoy a degree of icon stature, at least locally. Recently her focus had been on stopping seismic blasting.

"Laura, no one has approached me—our property is too narrow. Even if they did, I am not selling, and you and I both know that Maurice doesn't need the money and he wouldn't sell anyway. I didn't get this place to make a profit . . . well, yes, I was hoping to make a profit, but not by selling to some developer."

"Your heart is a good one, Dean, and you will be rewarded for that."

"Well, I have a lot to atone for . . . you look tired, Laura."

"I am," she confessed. "I am getting tired of fighting. Well, not so much the cause and I don't think I would be tired of the fight but it's just so unfair. It's all about the money. We can't even fight the fight because of money. They have so much and we have so little. I swear, Dean, if the money were even, I would not grow tired of the fight."

She said all this slowly and with real, deep feeling. I felt bad for her. She was obsessed and couldn't stop her obsession. I doubted she would ever feel she had succeeded or made a real difference. I both envied and pitied her. How great it would be to be so singularly obsessed with something. I suppose I was this way with football but not to the extent she was. That part I envied. I pitied how tired she was and the thought that she would probably never give up and never feel as though she had won. She was the one with the truly good heart.

We sat together for a long time, not really saying much. I refilled her mug and mine, put some UB40 on a low volume, and we just sort of relaxed in the warmth and wave sounds until people started showing up and I got busy handing out alcohol to happy people.

The day was very uneventful, with Rose showing up and assisting me. I was thinking a lot about Jaime. I knew he was on the run with a lot of Whitey's money.

I was wondering throughout the day where he might have gone. I realized I was losing my detective skills when I could not even answer the question as to whether or not Jaime had a car of his own other than the one he left at the club. I had just assumed that he did. Marcia had given me her cell phone but, even though it would give me a good excuse, I didn't want to talk to her until I knew something. I knew she would call me, at the bar or home, if she found Jaime or even found out anything that might be of importance.

I was wondering if maybe he went back to Pittsburgh. Most people's natural instinct is to go home, to go where it is safe. But, from the story Marcia had told me, Jaime didn't have much of a relationship with his family back home, and if Ralph, Manny, and Mookie were really, really after him, then Ralph knew his home was in Pittsburgh and if Whitey was big enough and this matter serious enough then Whitey could have anybody track Jaime down in Pittsburgh. Pittsburgh didn't seem right to me.

I was wiping off a table when Jerry came bounding in. He was scanning the room for Sara but settled on Rose.

"Rosie, my dear," he said in a singing voice as he hugged her. "I'm so happy to be back and see your smiling face."

Rosie wasn't smiling. She pushed him away while balancing a tray of glasses.

"Fool, I didn't even know you was gone."

"Oh yes," Jerry got serious. "I had a hot lead on a big business deal very late last night, jumped last second on a small plane this morning, flew to Atlanta only to find out that they pushed the meeting back a month. It's a project, Rosie, that if the variables would just stay the same, we could make some money."

I shook off the part about "variables staying the same" and was focused on Jerry relaying to Rosie that he had jumped, last second, on a small plane. I didn't know if Jaime had a car or not but I bet he had a small plane.

CHAPTER FIFTEEN

spent the next three days calling around, occasionally having Sara look some things up on her iPad, and then one day, I hit it.

I called Amphibians Plus, a small airport in Bartow, Florida. About three and half hours away from the Turtle and about three hours from the Lago Mar.

I was pretty much done with any standard line after striking out so many times, so when I called I just asked the person who answered if Jaime Devine was there.

"Jaime? Well no, I haven't seen Jaime since he took off in that new floater of his some time ago."

Although no one at the bar came over and told me, I am pretty sure my ears perked up; they actually felt like they did.

"Floater?" I said.

"Yep, his ol' floatplane, whatever you wanna call it."

"Did he say where he was going?"

"No sir, Jaime never says, just gets it and goes, but ain't never been away this long. Everything OK?"

"I think. . . . I haven't heard from him so I'm starting to get a little worried."

"Very true, we just been sayin' we wonder where he is, not really worrying about it. You his friend?"

"Yeah, we've been friends since college; Marcia's worried."

"Don't know no Marcia, that his girl or something?"

"Yes . . . did he go with anyone?"

"No, not that I know of—didn't usually."

"And you don't know where he went?"

"No sir. Gotta go."

"OK. Thanks."

Well, that was weird, but at least it got me going and I thought I should borrow the Thing again and head to Bartow to get some more information.

The drive to Bartow was nothing like the drive to Fort Lauderdale; there was no ocean breeze on this drive to the middle of the state. Although I was tempted to divert off and check out Kissimmee State Park, it was one of those drives that makes you wonder how people even settled in this part of the country. Like when I left Florida to play at Pitt. Some of those winters would make me think, if you were a settler back in the 1600s, and you spent a winter in a log cabin, nearly dying of no heat and starvation, how would you not, when the weather got good, say I am outta here and head south. That was an age-old question to me but my ultimate age-old question was which was best:

Eating great food when you are starving?

Drinking when you are dying of thirst?

Sleeping so comfortably when you are super tired?

Pissing when you are dying to take a piss?

Shitting when you are dying to take a shit?

Or sex anytime?

I couldn't answer, thus making it an age-old question. I figured it had something to do with the meaning of life. I was beginning to think that sex was the best because it wasn't conditioned on anything. The other things all had to be when they were at their extremes. But man, doing any one of those, when they were at their extremes, was pretty awesome. Oh well.

I pulled into the grounds of Amphibians Plus in the middle of the afternoon. It was scorching hot. I was not used to being in the Florida heat where there was no ocean around. No ocean breeze. The airport was small with one tiny sort of dirt runway. There was a good-sized hangar building but the place seemed pretty deserted. I pulled to a stop and turned down the Yellowman I was listening to. I still had a lit Arturo Fuente 8-5-8 going and, as I got out of the Thing, I was aware that I was sweating.

There did not seem to be anyone around. There were no planes taking off or landing. The whole place seemed deserted. I walked toward the big opening of the hangar. I could not see in as the hangar opening was not facing me but sort of sideways to me. I noticed an office door on the side wall and I decided to go there. I opened the door and surprised the hell out of two young guys smoking out of a bong. When I opened the door a little bell thing had gone off and the one guy who had about been ready to take a hit tilted and spilled the bong water totally on the other guy's lower legs and feet as he was still trying to light the bong. The guy spilling the bong was just looking at me as I came through the door. The guy trying to light the bong wasn't fazed by the bong water hitting his lower legs and feet (he had sandals on) and he said, "Man, hold it straight up," in a slow, stoned voice that comes from being slow and stoned.

The other guy just continued to look at me and in amazement said, "Thor," in a hushed voice.

I decided to take the initiative.

"Guys, look here . . . focus," as I held up my hand to get their attention.

The guy still trying to light the sideways bong looked up while still hunched over and the other guy still just stared at me.

The lighting guy when he saw me said to the other guy, "You know this dude?"

And the other guy without taking his eyes away from me said, "I think it's Thor and I think he's trying to hypnotize us."

The other guy then kind of yelled at me, in a pleading sort of way. "What do you want, man?"

These guys were really stoned.

"OK," I said. "I just want you to answer some questions"

"Oh, thank you, man," said the lighter guy, smiling, now feeling good and relaxed while the other guy just stared at me in some kind of disbelief or shock.

I puffed on my cigar as I didn't think they cared about the smell in this cool, dark office area.

"Do you guys know Jaime Devine?"

"Sure, man."

"Man, I gotta stop man, this guy looks just like Thor."

"Whoa, could you imagine, what if . . . he really was Thor?"

And, that was it. They started down a laughing path and I knew they wouldn't be back. So I went back out into the bright sun, leaving them behind while pulling the door shut. I was hoping to find someone else, and I did.

His name was Vernon. He was probably sixty-something, sporting a crew cut, and working hard on the engine of a brightly colored airplane. I recognized the voice from my phone call. Vernon and his wife, who was nowhere to be seen, owned Amphibians Plus. He asked me if I had met Dumb and Dumber and I told him I had. He didn't stop working on the engine as he talked with me, and I could tell by his hands and his apparent old-man strength that he had worked hard his entire life.

"They're good kids," he said. "My nephew and his buddy." He paused. "My nephew's been livin' with us since he was little. My sister, his mom, never did amount too much so we took him in. The kid can fly a plane like no one. If he had half a brain, he could do something with that talent."

Even though we were in the expansive shade of the hangar, it was hot. I was sweating. I had left my cigar on a cement block outside the hangar. Most times I didn't take a lit cigar in places where I wasn't sure they were welcome.

"Vernon, you mind if I get my cigar from outside and smoke in here?"

"Hell no, be nice to have a different smell than the weed the boys are always smokin'. You got one fer me?"

"Sure," I went out into the blistering sun and got my cigar and puffed on it as I went to the Thing, retrieved one for Vernon, cutting it before I headed back.

Vernon lit and smoked the thing like an old pro.

Vernon and I talked for a while. I handed him tools when he needed them and I asked him stupid questions about planes, but he did tell me quite a bit about Jaime.

Jaime had been coming there for about ten years. Vernon had even helped him pick out his first floatplane. Vernon could not remember when they first met. Jaime had upgraded; he bought another, better floatplane a couple years ago. He actually gave Vernon his old one, which Vernon pointed out to me in the hangar. It was a nice blue-and gold-colored plane. Vernon said he and his nephew used it to give flying lessons, if anyone wanted to learn to fly a floatplane. Vernon had helped Jaime pick out his new model and was not charging him for keeping it at his place. Vernon told me the name of the model, but I knew I wouldn't remember.

"What color is it?"

"Blue and gold, of course. Jaime insisted on blue and gold, said it was his lucky color combo. We had it sent to a painter in Georgia before it was delivered. I gotta admit, it did look dandy."

"Did Jaime come here a lot—did he fly a lot?"

"Not so much lately; he did when he first got that one over there. Came a lot back then. Lot of times, he'd come here as it was gettin' dark to take off right as the sun was setting."

"When did he leave this last time?"

"Don't know . . . came out the one mornin' and the plane was gone... we was expectin' to see Jaime come back but he hasn't."

"When he would go, how long would he be gone, usually?"

"Usually come back before sunrise. All very quiet stuff. No hidin' but not being real outgoin' either."

"Man, I wonder where he was a goin?" I found myself talking in the drawl that Vernon was using. If I stayed around here long enough, I'd either be wearing bib overalls and sporting a crew cut or be wiping bong water off my sandals.

"Don't know, never said, but I do know about how far he would go, same every time."

"How far, and how did you know?"

"Gas. Jaime be filled up before he left and then I'd fill him up the next morning. Jaime always wanted his plane full. Always same amount I'd put in there. Figure he flew about 400 miles or so each time."

"Do you know which direction?"

Vernon was pounding the cigar. Some guys smoke cigars really fast. I am sort of a middle-of-the-road smoker when it comes to time it takes to consume, but Vernon here was a speed smoker. I could tell he was enjoying it.

"Nope, no way of me telling that but he did some landing in the ocean. Could tell by the saltwater residue on Jaime's plane each time he got back."

I thought for a minute. Actually, found myself with my head lifted up toward the rafters of the hangar, blowing smoke out, contemplating.

"Vernon, any way of checking flight records or anything like that so I could see where he might have gone?"

"Nope, nothing I got here would help in that, but I got a buddy may be able to help you out."

Vernon put his wrench down, rubbed the grease off both hands onto his thighs, and went over to his bench area. He ripped a piece of light green paper from a steno pad, thought for a little as the cigar nearly burned his lip, and finally wrote, in cursive pencil a name, telephone number, and a short string of numbers and letters. He handed it to me.

I looked at it, frowned a little, and asked, "This is really the guy's name?"

"Yep, some kind a Middle Eastern shit but he's good people, he's a controller, knows all about flights, flight patterns, trackin' flights. I been knowin' him for a long time. Tell him I told ya to call on him. The numbers and letters at the bottom belong to Jaime's plane; give him those."

"OK, well listen, thank you very much, Vernon. I really appreciate it and I'll let you get back to work. Nice meeting you."

"Same." We shook hands. He had hands that equaled mine in strength and we had a good manly handshake. I walked outside to the Thing and decided to take two cigars back to Vernon; besides, as I was walking back a couple of additional questions occurred to me. I got two Oynx from my supply and headed back. Vernon was where I left him.

"Vernon?" I said to his back.

"Yep," he said without missing a beat of work.

"Here are two more cigars for your time and I was wonderin' … how many times did Jaime go and how was he dressed?"

As Vernon was reaching for the cigars, he said, "Well, thank ya. I'm guessin' he went five times since he got that there new one and nothing special in his dress, nothing special."

"OK, well take care."

"Yep, you do the same."

CHAPTER SIXTEEN

The heat was almost unbearable as I slid back into the Thing. I didn't want Vernon to see the Thing as I didn't think he would appreciate a yellow, flowered hippy mobile, although he was pretty liberal with Dumb and Dumber's smoking habits. The Steel Pulse music and the breeze, although hot, generated from my speeding down the lonely roads of central Florida were perfect for my Jaime thinking. What was he doing?

Hopefully, when I got back to the Island and called on Vernon's Middle-Eastern friend, I would at least know where Jaime had been flying to.

I got back to the Turtle as it was getting dark. My Corvette was parked in the El Jefe spot and I found Beans inside, at his usual end of the bar, so the exchange of keys was easy. The place was really crowded. Rosie let me know that there was some kind of big family reunion going on at the Ritz and the younger crowd had escaped the formality. I didn't need to tell her to make sure and card; she was much tougher with that than me, but I did remind her to remind Sara. Sara was terrible at carding people. Either she was afraid she might hurt their feelings or she just didn't remember. Rosie looked at me like I thought it was her first day on the job.

"Boy, now, you know I already had that talk with her."

"I know and as long as we haven't heard anything from Bob, we should be OK, even though half the group in here looks like they're underaged."

"Man Dean, we getting to that age where everybody be lookin' too young; you seen some of them doctors nowadays? Look like high school kids."

"True."

"Bob" was Sheriff Bob. Sheriff Bob had actually gone to school with me, Rosie, and Maurice. He was two years younger and in school always looked up to me and Maurice as younger guys often do with the older star athletes. Fortunately, Maurice and I never treated anyone badly so Sheriff Bob was a friend. Bob became sheriff at a young age. Even though he had a stomach on him now, he was still one of the younger county sheriffs in the state of Florida. Bob was a good guy and he knew that we were reasonable in who we served alcohol to. It was not Bob we had to worry about. It was the State Liquor Control agents we had to worry about. They would come in undercover and observe. If a bar owner sold to an underaged person, they would bust the underaged person and the bar owner. Sometimes they would even go to the extreme of having an underaged person working with them to come in and order.

With our place, all they ever got to do was observe. Out of professional courtesy, the agents would let Bob know when they were coming to little Fernandina Beach. Bob, in turn, would give me or Rosie a call and the conversation usually went:

"Well, hey Dean, everything all right over there?"

"Sure, Sheriff, how you been?"

"Well, I'm good, Dean, but you may want to button down a little over there as it's supposed to be a little windy tonight and maybe for a couple days."

"Thanks, Sheriff, we'll keep an eye out."

But, tonight wasn't proceeded by any storm warning from Sheriff Bob, and even though some in the crowd looked a little young, they all had adequate IDs or adequate enough fake IDs so that we were all comfortable. The vibe was great, the music, talk, and laughter a little louder than usual. I stood back and enjoyed the view. But my thoughts soon turned to Marcia and memories of the way we were.

Why was it that the reflections on the past brought back only good memories? Why did everything always seem so much better in the past? I was thinking about the days and nights we spent together. Marcia and I seemed like a perfect fit. Something that was meant to be. God, I had avoided dwelling on the past for so long. It was a shortfall, my Achilles heel. I don't know how much other people dwell on the past, but I had for an unhealthy amount of time in my not so recent past. I would dwell on the old high school days, but mostly on Marcia and the Pitt days. Moving back here, getting the Turtle up and running, and not drinking anymore really helped me. The past was the past, but Marcia was part of the best part of the past and now she was back. I shifted my eyes from the stare they were in and looked at a group of young family and friends. They were having a great time and I decided I wasn't going to infuse the Turtle with depression-based reminiscing. I smiled a sincere smile and moved over to be with my old buddy Beans. Beans, of course, greeted me with a blast I could hear even above the music.

We closed late, but I was up early. Lori had stopped in that night but I knew I would be late so I did not mention anything to her about coming over. That morning I was up and out the door on my run. I needed a run, mentally and physically. I decided to go without headphones, choosing instead to listen to the awakening of the small community. I headed down to the pier and caught the sounds of the fishermen heading out. I had a route of a little over three miles that I typically ran. It didn't take me near the ocean but it was a nice street and sidewalk route that got the job done. I was sweating heavily when I got to my place. I decided to have coffee on my porch instead of at the Turtle, so I showered, drank a protein drink, and headed down the block to Amelia Island Coffee. The girls knew what I wanted so I didn't even have to order. I did grab a *News Leader* newspaper to go with my large coffee and headed back home.

I sat on my front porch just thinking. Basically, I knew little about Jaime. I wanted to call Marcia before I called Vernon's flight plans friend. So I got the phone and dialed the number I had committed to memory.

She answered. She sounded nice and sweet.

"Marcia, how are you?"

"Dean, I'm fine. It helps to be here with Mom and Dad. I haven't told them that Jaime is missing, just that I wanted to come and visit for a while. But I think we are all pretending that they don't know something is wrong. I haven't been the best daughter for just wanting to come back and visit, you know."

"Well, Marcia, I am sure they love having you there."

"Are you kidding? Mom hasn't stopped cooking since I've been here and I have probably gained about ten ponds." She laughed a little and we were silent.

"Dean, have you found anything out?" "No, not really, Marcia, but I was wondering if there were a way I could get in your place at the Lago Mar?"

"Sure. I didn't do anything with it, just locked up and left. I hardly even took any clothes."

"OK, I just want to look around some more. Last time, my visit was rudely interrupted and I would like to see if I can find something that might give me some ideas about where Jaime might be."

"OK, please do, Dean. I'll call the management, tell them my friend is coming to stay, and give them your name. They'll have a key for you over at the hotel."

"Perfect. I think I'll leave a little later today."

"I'll tell them, Dean. And Dean . . . please call more often."

Either she meant to sound intriguing or I was reading way too much into it.

"I will, Marcia," I said in a too slowed-down, seductive way. Jesus. I just hung up then.

My next call was to Vernon's guy, the plane tracker. I looked at the piece of paper Vernon had given me, for the number. It was a Miami area code. As I dialed the number, I looked at the name again to make sure I had it right.

"Yep," was the answer.

"Is this Fuhhead?"

"Fuckhead; did you just call me Fuckhead?"

"No . . . Fuhhead is what I said."

"Listen here, you sumbitch, if you got any balls whatsoever, you come over here and call me that to my face." Guy sounded like a Vernon clone.

"Wait, wait, wait a minute, I'm looking for a Middle Eastern guy by the name of Fuhhead. Vernon, at Amphibians Plus in Bartow, gave this number."

"What the? Oh. . . ." followed by a burst of cigarette-smoking, hacking laughing.

When he had hacked his last few laughs the guy on the other end said, "Man, ol' Vernon got us both, I ain't no damn Middle Eastern sumbitch and my name surely ain't no Fuckhead." More hacking laughter.

"Jesus, sorry, man. I guess Vernon did get us, well me especially. Do you know about tracking flights and flight plans?"

"Hell yes, I was a controller till the replacement but I still follow all kinds of flights, do consultin' work and such."

"Great, well my name's Dean Hunter and I went to see Vernon about a friend of mine who had a plane at Vernon's but took it out and has been missing for some time. That's when Vernon gave me your number and the wrong name."

More hacking laughter. "That crazy sumbitch. You got identification of your buddy's plane."

"Yes, Vernon gave it to me. Ready?"

"Hell yes."

I read off the line of numbers and letters.

"Hang on, this'll be easy."

I heard computer typing in the background.

"Well seems your buddy used to like to fly to Freeport in the Bahamas pretty much but no flight plan in the last month. If he took off recently, he did it without notifying anybody where he was goin'."

"OK, thanks. Oh, what is your name, by the way?"

"Name's Billy. Bill McClain, not previously known as, nor ever hope to be known as, Fuckhead." More hacky laughter during which I said goodbye and hung up.

CHAPTER SEVENTEEN

As much as I loved taking the Thing for a road trip and as much as I knew Beans would have no problem loaning it to me again, I decided I would just rent a car. I put on another pair of running shorts, a Pittsburgh Pirates worn out t-shirt, and grabbed my too-big-for-Marcia bike and headed down the road. It was a haul to get to the Enterprise on A1A but I made it.

Well, I guess there is a reason people call in advance for rental cars. I had three choices: a mini cooper that I wasn't even going to try and get into, a hardtop Neon with no air conditioning, or a pink VW convertible Beetle. I picked the Beetle, white interior and convertible top and all. At least I could smoke my cigars (even though it was a nonsmoking car). I put my bike in the back and drove off, headed back home.

I packed like I did the last time and in the same mood. I discovered that it didn't take much to make me think I was going on a nice trip, a vacation-type trip, an adventure. I put the hard top on the Corvette, left Cari a note and a small stack of money (payment she would be expecting), and drove to the Turtle. Rose was there, staring at Larry from our front deck. Larry was maneuvering his metal trash cans around. I parked in the El Jefe spot and bounded out of the Barbie-mobile and up the steps. Rose didn't take her eyes off of Larry.

"Look at that ol' fool. Damn cans don't even need moved and he out there bangin' 'em around like it was the most important thing."

Just as I looked, Larry coughed and kind of caught himself. I thought I noticed Rose flinch a little. Larry looked up and flipped us off. Rose slapped the small towel she was holding against the railing and turned, exclaiming "fool" while heading into the Turtle.

I followed, letting the screen door slam. The fans were on full speed, the place was clean. Rose had come in early to clean the mess from the night before.

"Rose, I gotta go again. This time should just be for the night."

"Yeah, yeah, yeah."

I think Rose was still mad at Larry and I felt like a little kid asking for permission at the wrong time.

"You go on a head with yourself, Dean, shack up with Miss Fancy Shorts. Woman got you driving a girlie car and shit."

"It's a rental; it's all they had and besides, I'm not going to be with her. This is business."

"*This* is business!" Rose said as she spread her arms out and took in all the Turtle.

"OK, you're right, but I have to go. Look, I know you have been working hard and, if you want, we can just close it down for two days. I'll still pay you but we can take a break."

"Oh, Dean. That ain't it. I don't mind the work; it's not workin'. This the only thing I got, you know that. I just let Larry get to me. Man ain't got no right actin' that way to me."

"I know Rose." I gave her a hug. We hugged for a couple minutes until she dropped both her hands and squeezed my ass as hard as she could.

I jumped.

"Damn, that hurt. Jesus!"

She was laughing, and I was glad.

"Teach you to get all sentimental with me. Now go on, get out and chase your Miss Fancy Shorts. You know everything all right here."

"I know" I said as I reached over and kissed her cheek.

I don't know if people were staring at me or I just thought they were staring at me as I sped down the highway but I didn't pay attention. Let them wonder about a big-ass, cigar-smoking, pink-Beetle-driving guy. The car had a CD player but I had no CDs. It was constant radio station changing the entire way.

I pulled into the Lago Mar hotel in the late afternoon. I only intended on staying that night and the next (at the most) this time, as I knew I could thoroughly search Jaime and Marcia's place quickly.

As I pulled into the now familiar stone half-circle entrance, I saw Joey up ahead helping an older couple with their suitcases. I parked near the front sliding doors and went into the darkened lobby. This place had a definite soothing effect. There she was. I remembered Joey told me her name was Lia. The beauty behind the front desk. Come to think of it, I had never seen her anywhere but behind the front desk.

"Oh, hello," she smiled "We welcome you back?"

"Yes, yes. . . ." I replied. "Probably just for tonight and maybe tomorrow if you have something." I knew they did.

After handing her my never-charged-on charge card, she gave me the key and explained to me where to find the room. Seemed to me it was very near the room I had last time, if not that very room. I had already forgotten my room number for the trip before.

I walked back out to the car and gathered my things from the front. As I was opening the trunk to grab my smaller duffle bag, Joey came up behind me.

"Hey, Dean, nice pink car, should fit right in."

"What's up, Joey? Fit in? Fit in with what?"

"Lia said you are here for the convention next door."

"Convention, what convention?"

"The Flaming Flamingos of South Florida. They're having their convention in the condos next door."

"The Flaming Flamingos . . . what are those and why does Lia think I am here for them?"

"Man, the gay guys, you know the gay group of guys. They have a convention every year and here they are. There are tons of 'em, man."

I realized I did not want to be driving the pink beetle around the mean streets of Fort Lauderdale and was thankful that Marcia's place was just next door. The opposite side of the convention.

"Listen, Joey, you gotta tell Lia that I am not gay".

"Dean, no biggie. She ain't got nothing against gay guys."

"Seriously, Joey," I said with all seriousness. Not that I wanted to go out with Lia, just that I kind of took it personally what someone thought about me.

"All right, man, I will. You took care of me before you left last time and I guess I can help you out."

"Thanks."

"Why you come back so soon, Dean?"

"Oh, that reminds me," and it did.

I explained to Joey that Marcia called ahead and arranged to have keys to her place left at the front desk for me. He said "cool" and jogged off to see if Lia had them. I took a moment to survey the surrounding area. Last time Ralph and the blockmen had spotted me and my "hippie mobile" before I even entered Marcia's place. I didn't notice anyone this time.

Joey walked with me as I carried my bag to my room. We passed the pool area briefly and to me it seemed less busy. We headed up the partially enclosed stairway.

"Seems quiet here, Joey, we outta season or something?"

"Naw, just that a lot of families are avoiding us for the next couple days because of the convention next door."

"Really?"

"Yes, well, here's your room," he said as he unlocked the door. I put my stuff inside the doorway and handed him a five.

"Thanks. You talk to Lia for me?"

"Yeah, but she doesn't believe me." And he was off.

I tossed my stuff in the bedroom and went to the sliding door and opened it. The noise was not of children jumping and laughing but of dance music, laughter, and a very feminine male voice over a loudspeaker or megaphone or something.

"Now look at that shake, ladieees" I heard as I stepped out, and down by a tiki hut, in the condo area near the other side of the pool, I could make out several men (I guess) walking in high heels, bikinis, boas, hats, and so on, in what appeared to be a runway gay swimsuit fashion show. The high heels appearing to be too much, one of the guys, later loudly identified over the microphone as "Poor Jeffrey," rolled his ankle and went down. All the other contestants went to his aid while the microphoned host giggled away.

I watched for a few minutes, and then decided the balcony cigar smoke I had planned would turn into a smoke-while-I-walk-to-Marcia's-place smoke.

I smoked an Arturo and leisurely walked around the grounds of the Lago Mar and Lago Mar place. It wasn't too hot, and it was quiet. It wasn't yet sunset and I thought it would be easier to search if I went in their place before it got dark. I laid my lit cigar on the windowsill by the front door and easily opened the door with the key.

Knowing there was nothing to be suspicious of, I simply opened the door and turned on the lights. The curtains or drapes or whatever were partially opened so it wasn't as dark as when I had been there last. The place was clean and orderly and I felt as though I had no reason to believe that anyone had been there other than Marcia. I realized that there were a lot of questions that I had not asked Marcia that were probably very important. Maybe the time away from the detective game or maybe being preoccupied with Marcia had contributed to my neglect, but I could have had some basic questions answered: "Did Jaime say he planned on leaving you, Marcia?" "Did he say goodbye?" "Did he pack a bag?" "Did he say how long he would be gone?"

I knew it was "no" to all those, so maybe my not asking them was not that big a deal. I casually walked around the rooms, not really with any purpose. I wasn't in a hurry and I just wanted to feel the place.

I was never one of those detectives that felt as though the crime scene "spoke" to them. I knew a lot of dudes like that but that was never me. But, when I had the time at a scene, I did like to casually walk around. And that is what I was doing now. The place opened up into a large marbled floor living room area. I knew the feel of this marble from when I lay on it gasping like a fish. There was nice modern contemporary furniture, very sleek. The entire far wall of the room was a sliding door setup with a balcony beyond that and a view of the pool and ocean beyond that balcony. I walked over there and slid open the doors. The breeze was outstanding. This place could be very comfortable. It seemed cool, lonely, and quiet. I was not finding anything of value and was taking in the thought of spending time here with Marcia. Lying in bed, in the mid-afternoon, listening to sounds outside as a cool ocean breeze swept over us. But, I knew it was not to be—at least not anytime soon.

I made my way over to the pictures area, the landing spot for my sandal. All the photos were upright and I, again, was aware of the number of pictures of the Dominican Republic and the same beach area. Other than the DR, I could not identify any other of the outside locations Jaime, Marcia, or both Jamie and Marcia appeared in. I wasn't even totally sure it was the Dominican as there were no "Welcome to the DR" signs in the pictures. I began opening the drawers and was very surprised at all the clothing that remained, both of Jaime's and Marcia's. I resisted the urge to wear one of Marcia's thongs around on my head while I continued my search. I did not find any drugs, guns, or money. I did find an address book. An old-school, leather day planner thing. I decided to take it. It was clear that it was Jaime's and not Marcia's. There wasn't much in there but I thought I'd take a look at it later. I also pocketed a picture of Jaime. One I thought to be fairly recent. It was of him standing on a beach under a palm tree, leaning against an old beached fishing boat with a bright blue ocean in the background.

I sort of lounged around a little, helped myself to a bottled water from the refrigerator, and decided to leave. I was very surprised at how the place contained virtually nothing of interest. In fact, it was plain boring. I guess my place, if being searched, would cause the searcher to feel boredom but hey, I'm boring. I just pictured Jaime and Marcia as more of the jet-setting, swinger types.

CHAPTER EIGHTEEN

My cigar was on the windowsill where I left it and it was still lit. Quality cigars stay lit for a long time, which is a good thing.

I casually walked back to my room thinking it may have been a wasted trip. I hadn't gained any information. I didn't feel like spending the evening here in Fort Lauderdale, especially knowing that I shouldn't be driving my feminine car around while the Flamingos were all over the town. . . . What kind were they . . . what did Joey call them? The Flogging Flamingos, Flopping or Flocking? I couldn't remember and dropped it but then right away remembered Flaming.

I decided to lift weights in the Lago Mar weight room. So, after having changed, there I was in the seventies-style weight room, complete with Nautilus and Universal weights. Jesus, if you ever needed to film a movie or TV show that featured 1970s luxury, the Lago Mar was the place. It felt good to lift again. It had been too long. Sometimes, I felt I paid way too much attention to running and biking and not enough to lifting, even though I knew that it was equally important. It was just difficult to make myself drive myself to the Y in Fernandina, where I had a membership and where I actually enjoyed working out. There really was no excuse. I did a solid one-hour workout in the dark, small, carpeted, air-conditioned room to no music. My legs, shoulders, and arms felt the better for it.

I stopped by the restaurant area and picked up a bottled nonalcoholic beer that was very cold and drank it while I showered. I decided no dog discipline shows while here this time so I avoided the TV. Finished my beer, pulled on some jeans and an old Wrigley Field t-shirt, slid my feet into my sandals, finished the last of the beer, grabbed two cigars, and headed out. To where, I knew not. It wasn't dark yet but the sun was definitely going down. The breeze was nice as I walked by the pool area. Music played low and there were just a few people out. It seemed the pool party of earlier had taken an extreme slow down, and I suspected that everyone had gone in to recharge before heading out to the strip area of Fort Lauderdale. It was quiet as I headed to the beach, lighting up. I tried to think about what I knew of Jaime's disappearance, realized I knew little and began to think of Marcia and how I wished she were feeling the coolness of the sand and experiencing the soothing quiet of the late afternoon, low-tide waves with me. But, she wasn't, and I got back to Jaime and what I did and did not know.

He hadn't let anyone know he would be gone. Not Marcia, not Ralph, not Vernon, apparently not Whitey. Apparently, no one. His plane was gone with no flight info. He often flew his plane to the Bahamas area. He had Whitey's money and did not seem to care anymore about Marcia. At least I hoped he didn't care about Marcia anymore. Was there a chance he was keeping his distance from her for her own safety? I knew Ralph and his henchmen were looking for him. That I did know. After a short walk, I decided to head back. It wasn't very romantic, just me and my cigar walking the beach, and I wanted to take a look at that day planner to see if I could get anything out of that.

I was happy to see the day planner had been kept up; it appeared to be current. So current that the last entry was several days before the time around when Jaime had gone missing. It didn't have a time but it was the only thing written on that day, and it said, "get final coordinates from Roger." The day planner, as I leafed through it, didn't seem to have much activity in it but the "get final coordinates from Roger" appeared throughout the past year with about three months between each entry. I looked in the R section of the contacts but there was only Rafael's contact and some person named Robert Hilton.

Starting with the As, I made my way through. Like the calendar portion of the planner, there was not much content. Usually just a few names under each letter. Then I hit the Ls and the only name was "Lt. Roger Smith," listing his address as the naval base in Jacksonville and even had what appeared to be a landline number and a cell phone number. I deduced this because written next to the 904 area code number was the word "base" and next to the 317 area code was "cell." Years of detective work paying off, I decided.

My plan was to get to bed early and get plenty of sleep. I started that plan but either the Flaming Flamingos knew of my plan and were intent on spoiling it or they did not know of my plan at all. Either way, they carried on in such a fitful manner that I was unable to get a solid sleep. At one point during a brief deep sleep, I had a short dream that involved me being laughed at by Marcia and Lia as I wore high heels, a Speedo bikini, and a boa. Shutting the sliding door muffled the Flamingos' high-pitched cries and finally allowed me some sleep.

I was able to get up at an early hour, showered, and out of the hotel before eight in the morning. I didn't get a chance to say goodbye to Joey or wave to Lia, but I really wanted to get on the road. I had spent too much time away from Rose and the Turtle, and I really felt that I gathered all the information that I could in Fort Lauderdale. I was ready to get back to my routine and, truthfully, I was starting to wonder why I cared about even thinking of Jaime. Somehow I guess I thought my finding Jaime or at least finding out what happened to him would bring Marcia and me closer.

Cruising down the highway, I thought to myself, what did I expect? Did I really think that I would find Jaime or find out what happened to him and that would be the end of Marcia and Jaime? Would Marcia ever lose her feelings for Jaime, forget the many years that I was trying to erase?

Even if all that happened, what did I think would happen? What did I want to happen? Her to move in with me? I didn't want to think or dream about that, at this time. I just wanted her to want me, even for a short time. Like many memories of the past, time had made the past times even more memorable, more perfect. I wanted to be in bed with her, with just light sheets covering us. Even though our bodies had changed over time, I really believed that the memory of us in our early twenties would overpower any imperfections that may be a present-day reality.

I drove straight through, not even stopping at my favorite eateries in St. Augustine. I was very anxious to get back. I got back with no problem. I stopped by the Turtle, said my hellos to Rose and Jerry, hung around for bit. It was fairly slow. The Flamingos' convention did not reach up to Fernandina. I knew I had been neglecting the Turtle somewhat but we really paid Rose well and she lived for the place, so I didn't feel bad heading out of there. I wanted to get home and run.

I exchanged the pink Beetle for my car and drove in very macho Corvette fashion to my place.

As I jogged my usual three-mile path through the town, I thought about what I had found on this most recent trip. Lt. Roger Smith's name kept popping into my head. He appeared to be my only lead and he wasn't much of a lead. I thought I could get to him by trying the naval base and I thought I had something to talk to him about by referring to the coordinates language in Jaime's planner. And, again, I thought about the end game here; what was it? Did I want to find Jaime? Really? I didn't know. I just felt I was the only one with any ability or interest in helping Marcia. Ralph and the blockmen didn't seem to have good intentions, and I didn't know how hard or how far they would go in trying to find Jaime. Then I thought, what if they found Jaime? Would I know or would I continue to search in vain?

When thinking deep thoughts, a three-mile jog can go pretty quickly and easily. I was back at my house before I realized and ready to shower and relax with a fake beer. I was determined to get to Lt. Roger tomorrow, if he was in Jacksonville. I slept easily that night and awoke early. Back to the routine.

CHAPTER NINETEEN

The next morning, very early, I found myself rocking in a chair on our porch at the Turtle, drinking a strong coffee and smoking a strong cigar. I heard the labored sound of Laura coming around the porch. Minutes later we were sitting with our coffees, listening to the beach wake up. Laura was depressed and was talking about just giving up the fight and living like most people do, without making or even trying to make a difference. All this seemed to relate back to finances, and it wasn't small finances. Laura needed big money. I told her to keep the faith but I wasn't sure I was convincing. It's hard to be convincing when you are not convinced. Still, something had to come Laura's way. So much good in one person had to be rewarded, somehow.

I had Jaime's planner and after Laura shuffled off, I went into the Turtle and I decided to call the 904 land line number of Lt. Roger. A young woman answered in a serious southern drawl: "Mayport Naval Base." I didn't know what to say, I was caught totally off guard and couldn't believe that I had not thought this out. So, I said, "Oh, is this the Naval base in Mayport?"

"Well, yessir, that is why I answered the phone by saying Mayport Naval Base."

"Yes, yes, um, I have a friend that I believe is stationed there and I was wondering if I could come and surprise him with a visit; it has been many years."

"What is your friend's name?" she asked.

"Lt. Roger Smith," I said as casually as I could.

"Let me see" was her response and then there was some silence. Then, amazingly enough, she came back on the line and said, "Yes sir, Lt. Smith is here and you most certainly are welcome to come and visit him here at the base."

"Well, thank you very much and I will. Have a great day," I said with some genuine delight.

"You too, sir."

So a short road trip was in store but this time just about a half hour down south to Mayport. The Corvette could handle that; I didn't need to bug Beans for some form of hippie transportation.

I managed to get some work done before Rose showed up.

"Rosie, I have to head down to Mayport for a meeting; you got this here?"

"Man, if I didn't have this here, who would have this here? You off running around like Mr. Secret Agent Man."

"I know, I know. This will be over soon and I'll be back on track."

The drive was easy. I had made a reggae mix cassette tape years ago and that is what I was playing heading past the marshes toward Mayport. It was surprisingly easy getting onto the Naval base. Maybe it was because I had no ill intentions or more specifically ill possessions, because they did thoroughly search the Corvette and me personally. A very thorough pat down and a dog sniffed my car and me in every possible place. I can't imagine the nostril sensations that dog experienced. It probably would go back to the dog barracks and complain to the other dogs about how he had to do all the tough duty and that none of them had ever had to inhale the amount of cigar remnants that he just did. But I passed and after parking in the "civilian" parking spot assigned to me and being checked in at the front desk, I was being walked across the grounds by a young Navy guy. I didn't know what young Navy guys were called. "Soldier" did not seem right to me. Seaman, ensign, sailor. Anyway, we didn't have any conversation about it or anything else and we walked across crushed gravel to a huge grass and treed area. We stopped about twenty yards from the gravel end and the seaman or whatever he was stopped and pointed and said, "Lt. Roger Smith, sir."

"In the wheelchair?"

"Yessir."

"What happened to him?"

"Don't know, sir."

"All right, thank you."

The sailor turned and left me, headed back over the graveled area.

I watched him go and then turned toward Lt. Roger in his wheelchair facing away from me and apparently watching several sailors doing lawn work. I headed his way. The only sounds coming from the base were the gravel crunching under my feet and a distant mowing sound.

I didn't know exactly what I was going to say to Lt. Roger when I reached him but I was reaching him and for some reason thought that this would be an informative meeting. It was a feeling. He turned, but not much, as my gravel crunching got closer to him. He didn't turn his head around enough to see me and I could see why, as he had a very thick padded neck brace on his neck. His chair was the standard, old-fashioned, obviously government-issued wheelchair.

"Lieutenant?"

He just turned the upper half of his body in his chair so that his padded neck and head could be angled toward me.

"Can I help you?" he said in a very unfriendly tone. He wasn't intimidating in the least, just seemingly upset.

"Yes, I just wanted to ask you some questions about a friend of mine?"

By this time I had made my way to the front of his chair. He looked up at me while a very young-looking sailor sped around on a riding mower to the left and behind Lt. Roger.

"Well unless I know this friend, I don't think I can be of much help," he said with the unfriendly tone continuing.

The speeding mower was getting closer and louder as the boy sailor sped around in a large oval pattern.

"His name is Jaime, Jaime Devine."

He was caught off guard and I immediately knew he knew Jaime. Within a few seconds he had made up his mind to lie.

"Don't believe I know a Jaime Devine. Now if you don't mind, I'd like to get back to work."

So I decided to lie, knowing that I could lie with the best of them.

"Really? Jaime said I could come and see you."

He got visibly upset. Too upset, like that was the straw that broke the camel's back.

"What the hell about?" he almost shouted. "What the hell would a Jaime tell you to come and see me about and who the hell are you?"

I thought saliva was going to start spewing out of his mouth and his eyes, naturally bulging, seemed as though they were about to bulge out of his head from the anger. I remained quiet and just looked him. I had no answer for the "what about" questions he posed, so maybe I couldn't lie with the best them.

"Would you like a cigar?" I said in a calm, reassuring voice.

He looked as though he was going to break down and cry, a "the pressure has gotten to me" kind of crying. The mowing boy sailor seemed to be picking up speed as his oval laps were getting smaller, but he had a smile on his face and didn't seem to have a care in the world.

"We're not to smoke outside of designated areas, but what the hell, sure."

Ice breaker, cigars can be that. I took out one of the two small Macanudos I had in my front pocket along with some matches I hoped would still light.

"Sorry, they confiscated my cutter and lighter at the front gate." It didn't seem to matter to him as he was biting the

end off and reaching in his front uniform pocket for a nice
lighter. Not quite a Zippo but a high-end portable lighter.
Those who smoke notice these things. Within seconds Lt.
Roger had the cigar lit. He didn't offer the lighter to me
so I reached for it; he grudgingly handed it over. I made
a production of faking as though I couldn't get my cigar
lit. I wanted his mind to disassociate with handing me the
lighter. After I was lit, I pocketed it. Not cool among cigar
smokers, but I had determined that he was not cool.

He puffed, closed his eyes, and took a deep breath. I
wanted to continue on this relaxed pace while I thought of a
reason why Jaime would have told me to come and see him.

"How'd you hurt your neck?"

He looked at me but was calm. "Listen, I have had it
with this wheelchair, this neck brace, and having to supervise
this bunch of morons." He swept his arm about, covering
the four mowing boys that were working in our area. He
continued on.

"I can't believe the quality of young men the Navy is
allowing in these days. Morons. When I came, the Navy
had standards. Hell, the Army was where nimrods like these
four would have ended up." Again with a sweep of the arm
toward the four moronic nimrods.

"Well, whatever. I hurt my neck and my legs in a car
wreck. I was driving down the road and I saw a bumper
sticker on the rear bumper of a car in the right lane; I was
in the left and we were on a two lane, headed in the same
direction. It was a bit ahead of me. So, I see this bumper
sticker." He paused to puff some more. "And I was straining
to try to read it when I plowed into the car in front of
me." He shook his head a little. "Rear ended it, my fault.
Thankfully, no one but me was injured but I am sure once
they find out it was a Navy U.S. Government vehicle, they
will start to have neck, back, and headaches so much so that

they will have to run out and immediately see their lawyer . . . you're not a lawyer, are you?"

"No. What did the bumper sticker say?"

"What?" He was sort of daydreaming, thinking of something else. "Oh, yes, something about keeping your eyes on the road, not wrecking because of texting.

"Physically, I'll be fine. Just a matter of time until I heal up, but mentally, mentally they are killing me having me supervise these knuckleheads."

I looked over at the smiling, moronic, nimrod of a knucklehead speeding into another leaning oval turn on his mower just as his sailor hat blew off his head. He quickly made a sharp turn to retrieve it from the lawn, but the turn was too sharp and fast and he ran over the hat, spewing white material everywhere while the powerful mower made a shredding sound. Lt. Roger didn't notice, as this happened behind him, and he continued with his talking and puffing.

"They are just so helpless, God forbid we have to send these guys to war," he was saying as I watched the boy sailor, over Lt. Roger's head, figure out what to do. He stopped the mower and started his walk toward us. He came around to the front of Lt. Roger's chair, just as Lt. Roger was saying ". . . it's just that I'd be afraid for them . . . what is it, sailor?" The young sailor stood in front of Lt. Roger with just the band of his hat.

"Sir, permission to go to commissary for a new hat, sir."

"Jesus, son," Lt. Roger said while looking at me with an "I told you so" look. "I'm not even going to ask."

"Thank you, sir."

"Well, just go, sailor, and get yourself a new hat." The young man walked dejectedly off toward what I assumed was the commissary.

"Where were we. . . . Let's start with who you are. Who are you?"

I couldn't think of a fake name so I decided on the truth.

"My name is Dean Hunter and I'm a friend of Jaime Devine's. His girlfriend Marcia hasn't seen him recently and it appears that he might have disappeared. I'm trying to find him."

"Well, sir," he said as he took another deep puff. "That is almost a tragic story but I don't know a Jaime or a Marcia."

We sat for a couple minutes and I knew he wasn't going to start up with any conversation or that the silence would break him down into confessing that he knew Jaime. Despite the momentarily relaxation provided by the cigar, Lt. Roger was not a happy person and I had tried to make it sort of a motto to try to stay away from negative, unhappy people.

"Well, listen, if you should happen to remember anything about Jaime, you can find me at the Sandy Turtle in Fernandina Beach."

"Yep," was all he said and I headed back out the way I had come. It was pretty uneventful heading out of there, and all the way back to my seaside town I just thought of what little progress I had made. But I was certain that Lt. Roger was lying about knowing Jaime and I just could not figure out why he would be. There was something strange about Lt. Roger. His sudden calmness seemed fabricated; it seemed that he was a guy about to explode. Did Jaime's knowing Lt. Roger have to do with military matters or personal matters? Who knew? Not me.

I went directly back to the Turtle. I was able to relieve Rose and close out the night in a very uneventful manner.

CHAPTER TWENTY

It hit me in the middle of the night, waking me from a very sound sleep. I wanted to reach for the pen and notepad by my bed to write down things that I think of in the middle of the night so I won't forget but there was no pen and notepad as I always forgot to put one there. But I knew I would remember because I knew I was right. Jaime was in the Dominican Republic. There were too many pictures of him being there, too coincidental that he and his plane were missing. I knew I was right. The Dominican was one of those last frontiers where you could go to and blend in. Touristy enough not to be really noticed but remote enough not to really be found. I knew it.

By good fortune, Cari was scheduled to appear at my house for cleaning and lecturing the next day. After opening the Turtle and enjoying my routine while feeling smug about my detective powers, I headed back home to get some information from her.

"Why chew got a little sneaky smile on chour face?" she asked shortly after I appeared in my little castle.

"Because, Cari, I figured something out."

"Hmhm, like smoking the cigar is not good for your health?"

"No. Do you know anyone or have any relatives that live in or near the Cabarete in the DR?"

"Aw jess, my first cousin is the Chief of Policia in Santiago; it is not far."

"Do you think I could meet with him soon if I go to Santiago?"

"But, of course, I would love for you to. Choo could go to his casa, eat the best fruits and visit with his beautiful wife and five a childrens."

"Do you think you could call him now and ask?" My adrenaline was pumping. Pumping for what, I thought. To find Jaime? Man, my detective desires were much more powerful than I could have imagined. I wasn't even thinking of being the hero for Marcia. Wasn't concerned for Jaime's well-being. It was the thrill of the hunt. Finding the guy who thought he couldn't be found. I knew I was on the right track and I felt like going 100 percent.

Cari rooted around in her duffle bag of a purse and finally produced a small, very worn black address book. She flipped through the little pages with as much anxiousness as I had while mouthing names and phrases in Spanish.

"Ha!" she exclaimed. "He is right here," and she pointed very forcefully against the page she had found like she was proving a point to me.

"Great, let me see that so I can write his information down."

The name was written in a primitive-looking cursive but I was able to make it out and write down his name — "Bolivar Aguino"—his address, and his telephone number.

"Can you call him now, while I look for my passport and ask him if I come there if I could meet with him and ask him some things about finding an American who may be there?"

She was overjoyed. "I love my cousin and his familia," she smiled as she headed for the phone.

I went upstairs to find my passport. Although I was not a world traveler, I knew it was up to date as I often used it in Pittsburgh to go to Canada. I found it where I thought it would be and, as I came down the steps, I heard Cari talking a hundred miles an hour in Spanish on the phone.

She hung up with tears in her eyes. "You will be treated like the king. I lied of chew and esplained to him that you were the reason that Jorge and our childrens are doing so well in this country."

I felt kind of sad at that and I gave her a hug and she cried into my chest. I determined then and there it was time for Cari to receive a significant pay raise. I was becoming soft in my soon to be middle years.

I spent the next hour or so booking my flight to Miami and then Santiago. Next was the call to Rose.

"Now what you thinkin'?" was how she answered when I called her cell phone. Damn caller ID.

"Listen, I'm coming back to the Turtle to just check on some things and then I have to be gone again."

"Damn Dean, why don't you just elope and get it over with?"

"Don't worry, Rosie, we can talk about a pay raise." Jesus, what had gotten into me? "Or a title . . . a title might be better. How about She Who Must be Obeyed at the Turtle?"

"Just get your love-struck ass in here and give me a big ole kiss goodbye; you know all is well when the Queen of the Turtle is in charge."

So I killed some time at the Turtle and convinced Beans to hold up a little on the beers so he could take me to the airport.

I was feeling juiced at the Turtle. Excitement was overcoming me, and I turned up the music a bit with a selection that featured the tunes of Don Omar and Omega. Getting ready for the DR.

Beans took me in the Corvette, and I was thankful we had the T-Top off as he was in true Beans form. I regretted the time I presented him with a book by Benjamin Franklin extolling the virtues of flatulence. Something about the Royal Academy of Farting or Farting Proudly, something like that. Benjamin Franklin was Beans's hero now and justification for his continued "ass belching." He made me rip one before I got out at the terminal, insisting it was a parting good luck symbol.

And so I was off, or at least thought I was. Of course, it takes longer flying within the United States, even within the same state, than it does to fly out of it. My flight from Jacksonville was delayed forty-five minutes, which resulted in me missing my flight in Miami to Santiago. Three hours later, fueled by a Venti Starbucks and a CLIF bar, I was in line to board with a lot of very happy Spanish-speaking Dominicans. I was tempted to try to start up a pickup basketball game, as I was seemingly a foot taller than anyone boarding the plane. Once on board, the flight crew had a difficult time getting everyone to sit but eventually we were in the air for the roughly two-hour flight.

It occurred to me that I had not made any hotel reservations and of course did not speak any Spanish.

The airport in Santiago was very easy to manage. My bag was where it was supposed to be and customs was a breeze. It was hot. I had taken Cari's advice and not packed any shorts other than my swimsuit in order not to appear so much a gringo, even though I was clearly a big gringo. So my usual attire of jeans, worn t-shirt, and sandals seemed to put me right at home.

Once I grabbed my over-the-shoulder bag and duffel bag, I headed out into the late-night air. It was heavy and humid, but there was a lot of activity. I had exchanged my dollars for pesos in Miami, and I approached what looked to be a cab. It was actually an old Ford Explorer. The young man inside was blasting music but I got his attention.

"Downtown?" I asked.

"Sí, hablas español?"

"No," I replied.

"OK, OK, downown . . . el hotel?"

"Sí," I said.

"Cual?"

"Hmm, any hotel . . . nice."

"OK, OK, sí. . . . Mi nombre es Juan."

"Me llamo Dean." For some reason that was all I ever remembered from my Fernandina Beach High School sophomore year Spanish class.

I threw my bag in the backseat and sat in the front.

We sped off as fast as the old Ford could go and did not pay attention to any traffic signals or other cars. My driver occasionally politely tapped his horn to cause slower vehicles to get out of the way. He was young and wiry, and unfortunately, beyond exchanging our names, that is about all we could discuss.

Eventually we arrived in a very active busy center of Santiago. There were people out walking everywhere, scooters weaving in and out of traffic with several people on each. Music was everywhere. This city did not appear to sleep. I was struck by the activity. It seemed strange that at this very hour, on this same planet, at Fernandina Beach things would be winding down quietly and peacefully.

We sped by a brightly lit hotel. Hotel Century Plaza, I could make out. We went around the corner and down the block until Juan could pull over.

I sat in the seat until Juan pointed back to Century Plaza and said "Hotel?"

"Ah yes . . . sí . . . how much?" as I reached for my wallet.

"Novecientos diecinueve pesos."

He helped me extract the right amount and I ended up giving him 1,000 pesos. So, if my review of the money exchange that I conducted on the plane was correct, it appeared that I gave him a little more than twenty dollars. I had a feeling I would be taken advantage of a bit in the money department, but I was really looking forward to hopefully an endless cigar selection.

I had a smoother time at the check-in at the front desk. The guy behind the desk spoke English on par with Cari, and there was a room available for me. I threw my bag on the bed, located my cigar stash, selected an Onyx, and headed out. I was still too amped to go to bed even though it was past midnight. Once on the street, in front of my hotel, I lit up and surveyed the street. The crowd seemingly had died down a bit, and I walked toward what looked to be a convenience store. I bought a sugar-laced fruit drink and an empanada from a cart on a side street. I got momentarily off track down another side street as I ate, drank, and smoked. I was alone when I was approached by two imposing men. Both wore sport coats, and they stopped me in my tracks.

"Qué haces aqui?"

The other guy pulled back his jacket, exposing a revolver that was sticking out of the waistband of his beige Sansabelt pants.

With a mouth full of empanada and sugary fruit drink, the only thing I could think of was song lyrics I knew.

"Que tengo que hacer para que vuelvas conmigo, vamos a dejar el pasado atras," and I continued, "para mi la vida no tiene sentido."

They looked at each other and laughed very heartily. The jacket fell over the gun.

"My friend Dean, Cari did not inform me you were a comedian," and with that the bigger of the two finely dressed men stepped forward and gave me a big hug.

"I am Bolivar Aquino and this is my assistant Rolando Garcia."

I shook the heavy hand of the laughing Rolando.

"Well, I never did know what those lyrics meant; what did I say?"

"Haha, basically you said, 'what do I have to do for you to come back to me, Let's leave the past behind us, To me life has no meaning if you go' . . . haha!"

"Well, I'm glad I got my feelings out. Very nice to meet you." I was trying to conceal my sense of wonderment as to how they had found me.

"You as well, my friend, and thank you for being of such assistance to my beautiful cousin Cari and her family and for that I will be very grateful to you."

"That's kind but I am lucky for knowing her and being her friend."

"OK, now . . . we have a wonderful country with many great peoples but, my friend, even though you are a large gringo, you should not be casually walking these streets alone at this hour. We have followed you from the airport. It is now time for Rolando and me to walk you back to your hotel. We shall meet tomorrow—I will send a car for you at 10:00 a.m."

I wondered why they had followed me from the airport. Why not just walk up, say hello and give me a ride to my hotel? But, then again, I guess it wasn't my place to question how things were done in a country I knew so little about.

We walked the short walk back to the hotel, discussing the country and Bolivar's work as the chief of police for this big city.

Again, I slept like a baby, even in these strange surroundings. I was feeling very confident about finding Jaime, knowing that I would have the help of Chief Bolivar Aquino.

CHAPTER TWENTY-ONE

The morning came, and I had to jump out of bed and shower very quickly. As I was finishing my shower, I was regretting my choice of attire for this trip. I did not bring anything of note, nothing nice. Just jeans, t-shirts, sandals, some workout clothes, and tennis shoes. So, jeans, t-shirt, and tennis shoes it was. I thought sandals would be too casual as I thought Bolivar was the type who dressed nicely at all times.

The car was out front when I walked out of the hotel into the blast of hot, humid morning air. I was flagged down by Rolando. He rushed around the car to open the rear door for me. It was a black Chrysler 300 with extremely tinted windows. I looked in the open car door and, seeing no one, turned to Rolando and said, "Can I sit in the front?"

"Sí, yes," he responded, enthusiastically.

I got in the car and the temperature was an extreme change. Rolando apparently liked cruising the city in a mobile refrigerator. He was a man of few words. The city was hectic with few, if anyone, paying attention to the street signs or rules for walking. Scooters flew by and around us, sometimes with three people on one. There was a lot of honking but not New York City or Chicago honking. This honking was more like "I am improperly passing you and beeping so you know not to hit me as we both violate at least one traffic rule." It was very aggressive, friendly driving. It seemed if you could sneak in front of someone in traffic that it was more a tip of the hat to you by the person you snuck in on. The solid black vehicle moved easy through the traffic of cars, scooters, people, and bicycles.

After about a fifteen-minute silent drive, we arrived at a rather large stone and marble building that was extremely clean and well kept. There was a big black wrought iron fence at the beginning of a long semi-circular driveway. The gate to the fence was open and didn't appear to have a key pad or voice system but just an old-fashioned lock to secure it when shut. There was, however, a uniformed policeman sitting in one of those heavy, wooden, sloped chairs that are popular for porches of beach front homes. He was in the shade reading a newspaper and nodded at Ronaldo as we drove up. A big sign above the walkway to the heavy double doors announced Policía. Rolando parked at the foot of the steps and we got out at the same time. The blast of heat instantly warmed me as I waited for him to walk around the front of the car to where I waited. I looked up toward the sun and saw that there was not a cloud in the sky. It was a beautiful, bright day. When Rolando reached me, we both headed up the stairs and onto the walkway that led through a short courtyard area. I felt as though we were two dignitaries arriving at some summit, like there should have been press there waiting for us, snapping photos. The courtyard had a shaded effect so I went through a bit of a cool down from the heat outside the car, to the shaded heat, to the virtual ice box of cold air conditioning that hit us as we went through the doors. Man, these Dominicans loved their air conditioning.

The place was busy. There were uniformed cops all over, lots of keyboard action going on. It reminded me very much of police shows. Nothing about this place seemed modern. I noticed that most of the officers were carrying revolvers. We walked at a brisk pace all the way down the hall to another set of doors. These were not heavy glass like the front doors but instead wood. A brass sign to the right said "Jefe de la Policía Bolivar Aquino." Rolando knocked quickly and opened both doors, and I followed him into a massive office. Jesus, I felt like I was in some South American cocaine movie. The huge office, sharply dressed and manicured Bolivar and Rolando, me as the casual, sloppy dressed American in to report on business, and there was another man in the room who was fair, maybe European, and sharply but casually dressed. I felt as though I was way underdressed for this party.

"Aw, my friend, Dean," Bolivar stepped away from the sharp, casually dressed European-looking man and made his way toward me.

"Good morning, Chief," I said as we shared a strong handshake.

Bolivar turned in a sweeping motion from our handshake to take in the other man.

"My friend Dean, this is Inspector LaRacquet from Paris; he is our guest for a period of time that we are of hope is not so very long. Inspector LaRacquet, my friend Dean."

I was beginning to think Chief Aquino thought my name was "My Friend Dean" and was wondering if I should correct him.

"Nice to meet you," I said to the Inspector as we shook hands. He was the odd man out in the big hands, strong handshake club that the Chief, Rolando, and I had formed.

"Oui, pleez to meet ou."

I immediately wanted to ask him to say "hamburger," but I resisted.

"I am zorry, wat did ou zay was you nome?"

"My nome?"

The Chief let out a hearty laugh.

"My friend Dean, the Inspector speaks the many languages but English is not of his best. Haha, I thinks he ask what you say your name was?"

I knew why that was asked; the Inspector was going to check up on me.

I turned to him and said, "I didn't say but . . . Hunter, Dean Hunter."

"Inspector, I thinks we are over. Maybe we meet later should any news be developed."

"Oui," as the Inspector bowed his head. "Et waz a pleasure to ave meet you Mensieur Huntear."

As we shook hands again, I said, "You as well, Inspector" and I felt like I was taking on some sort of overly formal affect.

He left quickly and Rolando followed him out.

The Chief ushered me to one of the four huge guest chairs that were in front of his massive desk. I was beginning to get a little suspicious of the opulence. The personal maintenance, the sharp clothes, the obvious car, the ornate office, but then he offered me a big fat Cuban from the humidor, and the suspicion seemed to evaporate into the air as he cut the end. Besides, I told myself, he was highly recommended and related to Cari, and Cari was a saint.

Smoking in a luxurious office is nice. I was relaxed in the big guest chair, puffing away as Bolivar told me, like a school kid, making me promise not to tell anyone, that Inspector LaRacquet was Paris's most noted expert on the drug import into both the DR and France by and through Haiti. I confessed to Bolivar that I knew nothing about Haiti being involved in trafficking. He further informed me that he and the Inspector were working on a major cocaine chain bust that went through the DR into France. I told him that was interesting, but I thought to myself that he was sharing a bit too much information despite our pinky swear.

As we smoked, we talked about Cari and how she and her family were doing. He had a genuine love for her and I knew that was why he seemed to like me so much.

Finally, he asked, "And now, how can I be of help to you?"

"Well, Chief . . ."

"Bolivar to you, my friend Dean."

"OK, Bolivar. I am looking for an old friend. His name is Jaime Devine and I think he came here. He may have flown his own plane here. His plane is one of those little planes you can land on the water. I think or I guess I have a feeling he may be in one of the beach areas around here. I have this picture of him but I am not certain how recent it is."

I took the picture from my back jeans pocket. It was one of Jaime in shorts with shirt unbuttoned, holding a beer and leaning against an overturned fishing boat beside a palm tree.

"Aw, my friend Dean, I tell you exactly where thees is. It is in the beach we know as Cabarete."

"Perfect," I said. "How far is the beach you know as Cabarete?"

"It is approximately one and one half howers from this very location."

"OK, what is the best way for me to get there, as soon as possible? I don't want to waste time."

"I will have Rolando take to you to your hotel, you may pack your belongings and I will have my nephew pick you up and drive you to there. You will need these for this very important journey," he said with all sincerity as he handed me five of the big fat Cuban cigars.

I smiled and graciously accepted the gift.

"And please, carry this with you." He gave me his business card. "Do not be afraid to call me for any reason. My nephew will take you to a hotel that is steps away from the area in your photograph." I knew the Chief would help out with whatever I requested in my search and maybe there would come a time that I would need his help, his resources, but this wasn't official business and I thought I'd go it alone for a while.

Rolando was summoned, I went through the cold to heat to cold changes, and we rode to the hotel in silence. It did not take long for me to pack my few belongings, pay the front desk pesos, and find myself out in front of the hotel waiting for the Chief's nephew.

CHAPTER TWENTY-TWO

Wow, Chief Acquino's nephew Rafael was one ball of energy. He was about 5'4" and must have weighed around 115. He came screeching up in his red Toyota as I stood in the shade of the front entrance.

"You are the only big gringo standing in front of the hotel so you must be Dean," he said as he came practically running around the front of his car. He grabbed my bag and threw it in the trunk.

"Get in, we must get to Cabarete; there are many beautiful women there of all shapes and sizes."

His English was nearly perfect.

"Nice to meet you," I said as I scrunched into the front passenger seat.

"Likewise, and I am very sorry but my air conditioning is not working at this time," he yelled from the driver's seat to me.

His air conditioning was not working but his stereo was. Fortunately, I loved his choice of music. Raggaeton and it was actually a radio station. So, as we peeled out, the Don Omar song was ending and a loud male voice came on speaking the fastest, most enthusiastic Spanish I had ever heard. I wasn't sure I could take all this abrupt, noisy quickness. But then Rafael reached over and turned the radio down.

"Well, Dean, welcome to the Dominican. Have you ever been to the small town of Cabarete?"

"No, I haven't; well, I'm not sure. Maybe many, many years ago," I laughed.

"I do believe you would remember, Dean. The Puerto Plata area is very much unforgettable."

"Maybe I'll remember."

There was a second of silence and I wanted to talk more before he decided to blast the music again. We were darting in and out of traffic, occasionally emitting friendly beeping. I was not concerned and felt very relaxed and connected with the street life of Santiago. The city did seem big and crowded and chaotic but it flowed and there was natural beauty all around.

"Rafael, your English is outstanding; how did it become so good?"

"Ah, my uncle, Chief Aquino. He insisted that all the children in his family that he could influence become students of English. At first, I resisted, but now I cannot thank him enough. When I am in the States, it is easy to fit in."

"Nice. That is great that he insisted. I wish I could speak Spanish."

"My uncle tells me you are fond of cigar smoking. Please feel free to smoke in this car."

"No, that's all right—I don't want to smell up your car."

"Haha, I smoke cigarettes all the time in here, please."

The car did have a smoker smell about it, not too much, just a hint. It was clear Rafael took care of this car, but all four windows were down and he was in the process of lighting up a cigarette. So I pulled one of his uncle's cigars from my duffel bag that I had thrown in the backseat, cut it, threw the tip out the window, and managed to get the thing lit as we were heading out of the city at a very high rate of speed.

We spent the next hour smoking, jamming to reggaeton songs, getting screamed at by the radio guy, and hugging the curves of narrow roads through forested hills. The scenery was incredible. Beautiful countryside but populated by extreme poverty. We dangerously passed several old, nearly broken-down buses that were overflowing with people and sometimes animals. Children played by the sides of the road and most of the time when there was a house or shack very near the road, you could hear music blasting. It just seemed to me that the people I saw were very poor but very happy. So, maybe not really poor.

We entered in the Cabarete area. It didn't look touristy at all. More like a crowded little town. Not village-like but more like a town in the States that had narrower, busy streets and buildings close together. I couldn't see the beach or the ocean but it did have that feel. We parked right on the side of the road, sort of half on the street and half on the sidewalk. No one seemed to care. I got out and got my duffle bag and Rafael went quickly to the trunk and got my bag. He rushed past down about four steps, and I followed. He was at a desk of what appeared to be a lobby. It reminded me of a travel agency. The girl behind the desk was young and very disinterested. She and Rafael were having a conversation. The whole building, travel agency lobby and all, was white cinder block.

Rafael turned to me and said, "You can pay by the night and it will be two thousand three hundred and twenty-seven pesos a night."

I figured that to be in the neighborhood of $50 a night. Fine. I took out my pesos and handed the amount over to Rafael, who in turn gave it to the disinterested girl. Rafael got a key from her and went outside and up the steps and started around the building.

"My uncle said what part of the beach you are interested in and this place is right where you want to be. It is not the nicest place in all of Cabarete, but it is near everything and your spot of the beach will be right out of the door."

As we walked down the stone walkway by the building, the noise got louder and soon we were at the corner of the hotel that was at the beach. The beach was unbelievable. Palm trees, tables and chairs, people, and the bluest looking water that I think I had ever seen. A different blue than the waters in the Keys of Florida. This seemed to have several shades of blue and green. There were small fishing boats everywhere. A scene from a postcard. Rafael either didn't appreciate postcard scenes or was so used to this beauty that it did not faze him. We made a right turn and kept going down the path. When we got to the second door, he took the key to the doorknob. He opened the door as I got there.

One big functional stark but clean room. The door and windows were almost directly on the beach. There was a small refrigerator, a sink, and a table with two chairs, as well as a big enough bed and a bathroom with a small shower.

"This room does not have air conditioning, so you will be very hot. But there is a fan," Rafael said as he pointed to a big ceiling fan. The windows had big black bars on them that were apparently typical of properties in the DR. It seemed that homes had a lot of openness to them but then also had things like bars on the windows to prevent people and, I suppose, animals from getting in. I went to the window and pulled back the thin curtain. The whole beach scene was taking place right outside my window. This place was very agreeable to me.

"Dean, I have to drive back but my uncle said to give you these." He reached in his pocket and brought out a small flip phone and a business card.

"This phone is good for all of the DR. This card has all the numbers for my uncle and for me. If you need anything, please call us. Whenever you want to leave here to go back to Santiago, call me and I can come."

"Well thank you very much, Rafael." I reached into my pocket and pulled out the roughly 5,000 pesos I had set aside for him and tried to give it to him.

"Oh no, I cannot. My uncle said that you are special and that we are to treat you as such."

"C'mon, Rafael, that's a bunch of crap and I will be mad if you don't take it," and I practically jammed it in his hand.

He took it, thanked me, and explained that there was a grocery store down the street and that this was the last hotel before a lot of bars and beach cafes down this line of the beach. We said goodbye and he was off.

I didn't have much to unpack, so I threw my two bags on the bed and headed out to the beach area. There was a row of restaurants, bars, dance clubs, and cafes all down the beach. They were all somewhat in line and nothing was huge, so none seemed to stick out onto the beach area more than others. Even during this hot, bright, sunshiny day, it was cool walking down this row. The endless amount of palm trees provided the shade. It seemed as though each place was open to the beach with their side walls usually touching the neighboring businesses walls. Open aired, with cheap tables and chairs in front of each business on the beach, under the palm trees. A few of the real nice restaurants actually had roped-in areas with pretty nice tables and chairs set up on the beach. I walked slowly, smoking my cigar and taking in the entire beach scene. It was like a holiday. People were running in and out of the ocean, playing volleyball, walking along the beach, or suntanning. Both guys and girls had little on as far as bathing suits and there were plenty of foreign-looking, out-of-shape old men in speedos with a surprising number of beautiful, much younger Dominican women.

I bought some sort of yogurt fruit drink that had crushed ice and probably a lot of sugar, and I went out to a vacant beach chair and relaxed. I was tired and did not really feel like investigating but also knew that I could not spend a great deal of time here. I felt the vibration first, then the muffled ring of the flip phone that Rafael had given me. I fished it out of my pocket as a young Dominican woman went by in a less than skimpy bathing suit. I watched as

I answered. Before I could complete "Hello," I heard the booming voice.

"My friend Dean, how are you finding Cabarete?" I could picture the smiling face behind the voice.

"Oh Chief, I love it here and may never leave, and a big thank you to your nephew."

"Yes, he is a good boy, perhaps a bit on the side of hyper but good nonetheless."

"Well, he's been very helpful to me."

"Listen, Dean, we have the rumblings that there may be more than you looking for your friend Jaime and I want you to be careful, we are working on the confirmation end of what we are hearing and I will let you know as soon as we have something made of concrete. Now, I must meet with Inspector LaRacquet."

"OK."

"Please, my friend, keep the phone close to you and should you suspect anyone or thing, do not—for a moment—be of hesitation to call. I will be here."

We hung up, and I wondered if I was racing with someone to get to Jaime. I thought perhaps Ralph's henchmen had come down. I was tempted to call the Chief back and see if his "rumblings" might have involved a report of two human mailboxes plodding around, but I was enjoying the cigar, sugar drink, and the young woman walking in an obvious manner directly in my eyesight.

After about a half hour of her prancing seductively in front of me, I thought I'd be better off getting to the task I was there for. I pushed myself up from the extremely comfortable chair and winked at her as I was leaving. I was never much good at winking. I thought I usually over emphasized it, blinking too hard, and that is what I was thinking as I strolled under the palm trees, on the packed sand, and by the row of bars and restaurants. I came to a large open-front bar that was blasting American hard rock. I was drawn in with the prospect of maybe speaking English with someone other than the Chief and his nephew. The place was empty except for two young American-looking guys behind the bar. The place had a Canadian sports theme about it. There were hockey pictures, posters, and signs all over the walls. Very much out of place here. I approached the bar and yelled over the music.

"Hey, how you doing?"

"Great, American?"

"Yes," I yelled.

"Here, let us turn this down."

The one I was speaking with nodded over to the one who had yet to speak and that guy went to his end of the bar and greatly reduced the volume of the blasting stereo.

"Better," I said.

"Haha, yes we use it as kind of a filter. The only ones that will come in here when we are cranking it are those people that really want to drink in a North American place. Works great."

"Where you guys from?"

"Aw, Calgary. We left there twelve years ago on a day when the temperature was minus twelve degrees Celsius and we flew here and opened this spot. We haven't been back since. What can I get you?"

I felt obligated. "Well, you have any nonalcoholic drinks?"

"Haha, no sir, we don't. I can make you the fruit drink that we usually put rum into and hold the rum."

"Perfect."

We talked for some time about Canada, their adjustment to life in the DR, how much they loved it and had no intention of ever leaving. I got around to showing both guys (Dan and Jim) the picture I had been carrying of the older, out-of-shape Jaime, leaning against an overturned white, wooden boat under a palm tree with a beer in his hand. They did not recognize him but felt that the picture probably was taken on this beach.

After they warned me to try to stay away from the extremely attractive Dominican women that were barely wearing anything on the beach, I finished my second fruit drink of the day and overpaid them, telling them I would probably be around a few days and would stop back. As I was walking out the open end of their bar onto the beach, they cranked up the music again.

CHAPTER TWENTY-THREE

The beach seemed to have more of the beautiful women than before. Maybe it was because I was still aware of what the guys had told me and therefore the women seemed to stand out more, wearing little as bathing suits. Kind of like when you buy a new car, then you notice that same make of car everywhere. The guys said these women were referred to as "sanky pankies." Not quite prostitutes but willing to get with a foreign man, preferably a wealthy one who would at least spend lots of money on them and, at most, offer to whisk them off the island and to the wealthy guy's home country. Some of these women had virtually no chance of getting off the island and experiencing all the wonders of material overindulgence. I was certain I stood out as a foreign guy but not certain I had the air of a wealthy foreigner. I didn't have a beer belly and was not wearing a speedo, a gold chain, and a Rolex. Even if I did look like a plane ride out of the DR, I'm certain if one of these sanky pankies found out that I lived in a tiny home in Fernandina Beach, they would move over to the next guy who may be from New York City or Paris or London. So I was just strolling down the beach, painfully aware that I wasn't going to be engaging in sanky panky with any of the sanky pankies.

Walking around the beach, flashing the picture of out-of-shape Jaime was surprisingly wearing. I went to bed early that night and listened all night long through the barred open windows to the continuing thumping of the Raggaeton music.

I woke early and found a little spot that served coffee and some sort of breakfast empanadas. My breakfast was excellent. I was coming to the realization that I was getting nowhere in my search for Jaime and was thinking that this had all been a sort of pipe dream. What was I gonna do? At the best, find Jaime—then what? Obviously, he did not want to be with Marcia or he was trying to protect her by getting away from her. Either way, I wasn't going to be the knight in shining armor and bring him back and everything would be fine. Even if that were the case, what did I get out of it? Marcia and Jaime would be back together. Maybe I was hoping to find him living in a lavish beachfront home and with a harem of sanky pankies and I could report back to Marcia that Jaime was a worthless, sanky-panky-loving son of a bitch and Marcia would welcome me into her arms, and then into her bed. Still, I could not figure out why I was doing this. I thought an early morning beachfront cigar pontification moment was what was called for.

During my walk to the beach area, I noticed people sort of noticing me. I know that I was a little different, the big gringo in jeans, sandals, and a t-shirt. Also, I think I was taking on a sort of stature with the local shop and bar owners and even the sanky pankies as a result of my coconut catch.

The day before, I was walking on the beach and, as I was passing under a huge palm tree, I sensed a dark object coming from above toward my head. I didn't really have time to look up but instinctively put my hands out like I was catching a punt. Just as I got my hands out, a football-sized coconut landed perfectly in my hands and I held on to it, like fair catching a punt. Turns out quite a few of the beach people saw this and the tale of this was spreading. I guess falling coconuts hit people often and sometimes kill them. So, this was a little victory, a stick-it-to-the coconuts type of thing. I just walked casually to my room carrying the coconut while tourists and sanky pankies alike watched me go. A smooth move. Anyway, I was quickly becoming a figure on this beach. God, today was going to be a hot one.

As I was about to sit down, my little flip rang.

"Aw, my friend Dean, I am so happy to have catch you."

"Good morning, Chief, how are you today?"

"I, myself, am fine. However, I do have some fear for your safety."

"Don't worry, I'm pretty good at catching the falling coconuts."

"Haha, they can be a bit of a danger to you. Someday I will have to explain some stories to you about the coconut falling on some of our peoples, but for now, I must tell you that we have received word that there is a gringo arriving in the town yesterday, asking about another big gringo. We are of the belief that you are the big gringo that he seeks."

"Hmm, do you know what this guy looks like?" I was expecting to hear that he looked like one half of two moving U.S. mailboxes.

"We do not but believe his eyes appear to be large. We are checking the passports that have come in in the last forty-eight hours. We will let you know the very instant we find out. So please be careful, my friend, and notify me if you need my assistance. Perhaps my nephew Rafael should deliver a handgun to you?"

"Oh no, Chief, it has been so long since I used a handgun, I wouldn't know how. I think I could throw a coconut pretty good if I had to."

"Haha, my friend. I must go, business does not sleep."

"OK, Chief, thanks for the heads up."

I dozed off in the lounge chair that I'd been sliding into when the Chief had called. I couldn't help it, as there was shade under the palm tree. I had scanned the branches above before lying down as I didn't want a coconut falling down on my crotch as I slept.

The warning from the Chief didn't scare me. I figured it was Ralph's blockmen following me and I didn't believe I had anything to worry about from them. It would be kinda nice to catch up with them, smoke a cigar, let them know how much a loser Ralph was in college, and team with them in trying to find Jaime. The only thing that tugged at me a bit was the lack of physical description the Chief had. So, somebody tells him there was a gringo looking for another gringo. Whoever was talking to the gringo or may have been told about the gringo would have undoubtably been told about the U.S. mailbox appearance of the gringo, if it had been one of Ralph's blockmen, and I could not picture one of Ralph's blockmen without the other—the Chief had just mentioned one gringo. So I was thinking the one gringo must have been a pretty nondescript guy. In my experience, nondescript guys often were the most dangerous. But I found myself dozing off with visions of sanky pankies in my head.

Man, I was in one of those sort of half deep sleeps, very comfortable and relaxed. I was drifting in and out of dream scenarios. I heard beachgoers in the background as I dreamed of throwing a coconut at a low-flying plane and actually hitting it, causing it to crash in the distance, after which I ran away. As I was running, hoping no one saw me throw the coconut, I felt someone or something pulling on my shoulder. The pulling was getting more intense and I became aware of crossing over from dream to reality. As I was waking up, I still felt the tug on my shoulder. There was a face near my face as I was coming to, back to reality.

"Hey Dean, Dean, wake up, wake up."

The shaking continued on my shoulder and my head shook limply on my neck. I turned and within inches of my face was the face of Dan or Jim; I couldn't remember which was which, but it was one of the Canadians.

"Un," I managed.

"Dean, listen man, listen."

There was some urgency in Dan/Jim's voice so I accelerated my return to the real world by sitting up, almost at attention.

"What man, what?"

"Hey, hey, that picture, you got that picture you was showin' us?"

I reached slowly into my back jeans pocket and pulled out the crumpled picture of out-of-shape Jaime standing by the boat under the palm tree with a beer.

Dan/Jim held up the picture, straight out in front of our faces. Almost like we needed it extended in front of our faces so that we could focus on it. Our heads were inches apart, staring at the picture.

"Look man, look, hahahaha."

I couldn't figure out what looked so funny. Then I saw it, him.

Immediately to the left of the crumpled picture was almost the exact same image in real life. Jesus, it was Jaime, standing against the exact same boat, under the exact same tree. I hadn't even noticed the boat and tree before. Jaime wasn't wearing the same clothes and he didn't have a beer, but it was the same otherwise. Jaime was facing us. He didn't notice me sitting up on the lounge chair with Dan/Jim kneeling beside me with his arm outstretched forward.

"Oh my God" is all I could say in disbelief.

"Hahahaha!" continued Dan/Jim. "Fuckin' crazy, isn't it?"

"Wow."

"Hahaha, yes. Dan saw the dude walking down the beach and I came out here looking for the legendary coconut catcher, hahaha!"

So, this was Jim I was dealing with.

"Jim, thanks, man, and tell Dan thanks. I gotta go talk to this guy."

"Sure, man, hahaha! Let us know how this shit turns out. Stop by for a fake beer, we got it for you. Go get him, coconut hands."

I wasn't paying attention to him and already had forgotten if he was Dan or Jim.

"Yeah, yes, will do," I quietly said under my breath as I was pushing myself up off the chair with my gaze focused on Jaime. It was like I couldn't let him out of my sight. Like I had just seen an endangered species and I needed to keep my eyes on him, like he was going to quickly dash off into the bush and I would never see him again. I got my leg over the width of the chair and was standing facing Jaime. He did not look as though he were capable of quickly dashing off into the bush or that he had noticed me. Even if he noticed me, I doubt that he would quickly associate me with a search-and-rescue mission tied to Marcia.

CHAPTER TWENTY-FOUR

gathered myself, stretched the kink out of my neck, and decided I would stroll casually up to Jaime. The photo was back in my hip pocket but it was truly amazing how similar the live situation was to the photo. How had I not noticed this overturned fishing boat under this very palm tree and, what the hell? Was this some sort of Jaime hangout? Standing the same way, just sans beer. I was walking toward him and he was looking in my general direction but still was not focused on me as though he were searching for someone up by the bar area. His gaze was sweeping and finally landed on my walking stare. His gaze stayed on my eyes for a second and moved on. I didn't picture him turning and running. Even if so, he was never able to outrun my grasp during inter squad scrimmages when he was in his best shape in college, and I was certain he couldn't escape me now.

I was close to capturing the White Elephant. Was it the White Elephant that was hard to get captured or didn't appear? And did White Elephants have sales? I shook the White Elephant thoughts out of my head and continued toward Jaime. It was amazing how close I got to him before he actually really looked at me. He looked at me with a sort of "may I help you?" kind of look. His face whitened as I said, "Jaime?"

Either he was not quick-thinking enough or he wasn't trying to hide it, but right away he said "Yes?" but still showed no recognition of me. I was thinking if I would recognize him if I didn't know I was looking for him. I don't think so. I wouldn't have been expecting Jaime Devine to just show up in front of me at some remote tropical island. It was clear he did not know who I was.

"Jaime, Dean, Dean Hunter." It was funny watching the name go in his head, seeing his eye awaken, then place the name and then his big smile. Man, he still had the electric QB smile. He smiled a full second more. A warm smile, looked me deep in the eyes and reached his hand out in a shake while saying, "Goddamn, Dean . . . what are you doing here?" The move to shake hands turned into a hugging motion and I instinctively hugged back.

"Man, Dean, hell, you could still play. All in shape and shit."

"Ha, I don't think so. Those kids are too big today to be running around on a field with."

"Well the hell, what are you doing here? Vacation?"

"No, Jaime, actually I'm here looking for you."

"What, wait, whoa," he said as he slowly stepped back with his hands raising up as though I were pulling a gun on him. "Did Whitey send you?"

"No, Jaime, Marcia did."

His face saddened. He looked embarrassed and sad. He looked down like that news had just caused him pain.

"Jesus, Dean, I didn't want to hurt her but I had to do this."

"Jaime, let's go talk. Let's catch up. We can talk about everything."

"No, no, I can't. I mean I'd love to but I can't right now. I'll get a hold of you, where you staying? I'll get a hold of you."

He was suddenly very nervous, almost afraid.

"Listen, Jaime, I'm staying right there," and I pointed off in the distance to my place. "But I want to leave soon. I want you to tell me what you want me to tell Marcia. I don't want to stay here past tomorrow so I need to know."

"OK, OK, this is some heavy shit. I need to think." He was grabbing his head as though this was too much, like he had a migraine or something. "Look, Dean," he was almost pleading with me, holding onto my arm. "I need to think, I will get back to you, I promise. I want you to talk to her. I want her to know. It's important to me. I'll be back."

And he headed off down the beach. I considered following him but that would have been pretty weird. There was nothing to hide behind, no palm trees to run between and hide behind, and I would have just been following him down the beach. So I stood there and watched him go.

He went way down the beach near the bend, occasionally looking back, and then he headed up the beach into the area that had buildings. I just stood there. I didn't know if I would see him again. If not, what would I tell Marcia? Yes, I found Jaime. It was nice to see him. He seemed happy to see me. And, oh yes, we didn't really talk about much and he left. Great. Some detective I was. I didn't really want to stay around. I wasn't going to keep looking for him. I would give him through tomorrow to get a hold of me and then I was out of here. I began to think again about what the hell I was doing. I was in the Dominican Republic, not getting paid, trying to talk to some apparently crazy guy, and neglecting my business back home. For what? To be the white knight to some woman who clearly placed me in the number two spot. Then I started to wonder if the White Knight ever saw the White Elephant or ever went to his sale.

I sort of aimlessly wandered around. It seemed the sanky pankies were out in full force. I was beginning to long for some female companionship and started to worry that if I hung out here too long, my sanky panky resistance would not hold up. I could tell the strength of resistance was starting to dip to a dangerously low level because I was noticing the pankies with more interest. I wandered around, half-heartedly thinking about what I was doing. If I had to leave now, I would consider my self-imposed mission sort of half accomplished. I had located Jaime and he was fine. Well, at least he appeared to be fine. Well, at least he appeared to not be in danger. Hell, I don't know what he appeared. But I had found him which, if you think about it, was a pretty big accomplishment. All I had to go on, literally, when I began this less-than-adventurous adventure, was a picture. Now I had found and talked to him. So why didn't I feel more accomplished? I could go home now, tell Marcia I found him, talked to him, and told him she wanted me to find him. I didn't feel as though I had really accomplished anything, and if he didn't get back to me, I wasn't going to stay. That would have to be my report to Marcia. My aimless wandering had taken me down the beach beyond the point that I thought I had seen Jaime leave the beach. The beach seemed to go forever and my thoughts took me to the "What's the point of what I am doing in my life?" but always a reflection back to Marcia. Back to the carefree days of Maurice and me leaving for Pitt football together, full scholarships. Back to seeing Marcia for the first time. Such a clear memory.

I found myself nearly back to my place. I ordered some type of fruit drink at the bar closest to my place and decided to head back to my room. I was getting bored. Bored and mad at myself. Mad at myself for being here chasing Jaime. All in some weird concern for Marcia. Marcia, who was more concerned for Jaime. These thoughts were in my head as I went through the motion of unlocking my door. They were still in my head as I was pushed through the door and heard it slam behind me. Pushed may be too strong a word. I was pushed but it wasn't forceful. More like a "hurry up and get in the room" kind of thing. I did almost spill my drink.

I turned around slowly; it was Rafael.

"Rafael, what the . . . ?"

"Shhh, Dean, we believe you are being followed, tracked down, something like that."

"What do you mean followed, tracked down?"

"We know that a gringo came to town specifically looking for you and we are not sure, just yet, who that gringo may be."

"Well, do you guys have some sort of description or something?"

"Just that he has bulging eyes."

"Bulging eyes?"

"Yes, the kind that you would see on a Chihuahua."

"The kind you would see on a Chihuahua?"

"Yes, like on a gecko."

"A gecko?"

"Like on those tree monkeys."

"Tree monkeys?"

"Don Knotts, Marty Feldman, Steve Buscemi. . . ."

Just then, my closet door swung open. "All right already. Jesus, Marty Feldman. My eyes aren't like that. What the hell is this?!"

Screaming was Lt. Roger and he was apparently furious about the eyes comments. He was there, still in full neck brace, with his hand in the right pocket of his light jacket with his pocket pointed at us. It snapped me out of my wondering-how-Rafael-knew-so-many-bulging-eyed-actors thought.

"Rafael!" I said incredulously. "The man has a neck brace on the size of a mattress and you guys are focused on his bulging eyes?"

"My eyes are not bulging!" He really was furious.

Lt. Roger stood facing us with his hand in his pocket extended in our direction.

"Never mind," he said "Don't move; we need to talk." The anger still present.

"C'mon, man. That's the oldest trick in the book, finger in your pocket to make it look like a gun," I said.

At that, Lt. Roger pulled out of his pocket what looked to be a little Derringer-type handgun but a gun nonetheless.

"OK, hey listen, if it's about the lighter, I'll get you a new one."

His face was puzzled for a second. "You bastard."

"Who is this man?" asked Rafael.

"Rafael, Lt. Roger. Lt. Roger, Rafael." I made the introductions.

"All right, enough." Lt. Roger's voice had elevated a level. "What the hell are you doing here?" he asked me very directly.

"I was just groovin', until you put that gun in my face."

"Very funny, I know you're here looking for that bastard, Jaime."

"Well, why'd you ask what I was doing here and I thought you didn't know Jaime?"

"Oh, I know Jaime and that son of a bitch has my money; where is he?"

I didn't respond and he yelled, "Where is he?!"

He was getting overly heated. With his bulging eyes and constant scratching and pulling at his neck brace, he appeared on the verge of losing it. It almost seemed as if the mattress around his neck was tightening; his face was getting extremely red. He was boiling. I had been around plenty of guys who were gonna blow, who couldn't take it anymore, and he certainly looked like one of those guys. Whatever rope he had, he was at the end of it. I didn't know if Lt. Roger was capable of shooting someone but I wasn't really in the mood to find out. I trusted Rafael to be quick enough to be able to handle whatever course I chose to take and Lt. Roger's irrationality was really getting to me as he yelled, "Where is he?!" more than once in a desperate, high-pitched, red-faced burst. I thought this would be a good time to get information on Jaime and the money, but I really thought Lt. Roger was over the edge. He was going to blow and I was worried Rafael might be his target.

Having put my drink down, I was standing beside the only table in the little room and on top of the table within reach was my trophy coconut. I grabbed it and fired it sidearm at Lt. Roger. I'm not sure what part of him I was aiming at but the coconut hit him square in the face and the gun immediately went off.

Rafael was quicker than I thought. He was out the door as the stray bullet shattered the window near my head, and I burst through the door right after Rafael. Rafael sprinted left and I followed. We sprinted for what seemed to be a mile in and out of the bars and restaurants of the Cabarete area. People's heads were turning and watching us fly by, looking back to see what or who we were running from. The gunshot had produced some screams but only very near my room as we ran by. The music and activity on the beach was enough to muffle it further away. I did pretty good keeping up with Rafael, but he was young and quick and I eventually had to call out to him to slow down. Stop.

I didn't think Lt. Roger was following us as I was pretty sure the coconut to the face would have caused some damage. I doubt he would have shot us and perhaps I overreacted. I was certain once that gun went off, with the explosive noise and the shattering window, Lt. Roger had gotten out of there too.

"Listen, Rafael, I don't think he's coming," I said, trying to catch my breath.

We sat at a plastic table, sweating and breathing hard. A waiter came and Rafael ordered a beer and I got a nonalcoholic one.

"Man Dean, you fired that coconut at him. I could feel you were going to do something," he laughed, "but a heads up would have been nice."

"Yeah, sorry about that."

"Well. It worked out for us. I must call my uncle to report this."

As he was dialing the numbers, he said, "Man, I cannot believe how loud that gun was."

"Yeah, it was for a little shit of a gun," I said as I took a swig on the fake beer. It felt good, almost like a real beer, and I still had a bit of an adrenaline rush going on.

"Man, that Lieutenant's face is going to be messed up."

Then Rafael broke into a very rapid Spanish as his uncle must have answered and I could tell from some of the words and his exaggerated hand and arm motions that he was describing the way the whole thing had played out.

Finally, he ended with a lot of emphatic "sí"s.

"My uncle said that is the man that they were aware of as being here and looking for you. After I described his taking the coconut to the nose, my uncle laughed and said that you were a man that should never be underestimated. He also said that this gringo will be easy to find because it sounds as though he will need medical treatment, and a gringo with those bulging eyes and a big taped-up schnoz should be easy to find."

"Jesus, can't you guys see that huge neck brace he wears around his neck—why is that never a part of his description? The damn thing is the size of a twin-bed mattress."

"Haha, I guess that too. Poor guy has a lot of problems going on with him. You know about this money he was talking of?"

"No. But it has been mentioned before with Jaime. I have a feeling Jaime may have a lot of money that other people think belongs to them."

CHAPTER TWENTY-FIVE

was certain that Lt. Roger was not part of Ralph's group, but how was it that Jaime seemed to have money that belonged to Lt. Roger and Whitey? What was the connection?

We talked some more. Small talk, reliving what happened. The way you do after a fight or a football game. We were still operating under adrenaline, it seemed.

"Man, Dean, you cannot go back to that room tonight. Stay with me at the hotel. The accommodations are wonderful and there is a pullout bed in the studio area."

"Yes, Rafael. I believe you're right. Let's have another beer, settle down a bit more and make our way back."

We headed back, walking down the beach, back toward my place. I think some people noticed us walking casually back after having seen us sprinting by them a bit earlier. We had to pass my room on the beach to get to where Rafael was staying. As we got near, we saw some commotion near the doorway to my room and noticed that it was the local police, so we decided to head up there. I seriously doubted that Lt. Roger was hanging around. The thought that I had perhaps overreacted was starting to get to me, but Rafael didn't think I had and I remembered how I seriously felt Lt. Roger was about to blow a gasket at the time. Oh well.

Rafael seemed to know the two cops and he took charge. He explained to me that they were treating it as a crime scene; it would take a while to replace the window and that I should get whatever I needed out of the room. I felt as though I was in some type of show as a lot of tourists and locals had gathered around and really the only thing to watch was me gathering up my things. I left the coconut on the floor of the place.

As I walked out I gazed quickly at the faces, making sure Lt. Roger was not around. He wasn't. Just the usual crowd, but I did notice a tall thin man with sunglasses and a serious face watching from a bit of a distance. Instinctively,

I didn't focus on him as I thought he was focusing on me. But I did notice him and I did feel something was different about him. We headed out, through the same gathering of people. Apparently, the local police had not mastered the "move on, folks, there's nothing to see here" phrase. As we headed down the beach toward Rafael's place, I continually glanced back. It didn't appear anyone was following us but I couldn't shake the feeling that something wasn't right. It seemed there was a strange feeling in the air. It didn't have anything to do with Lt. Roger. The darkness seemed darker than it should have been, with a touch of fog or haze, it seemed.

I was a bit jealous when we arrived at the obviously touristy resort where Rafael was staying, but then I realized that I would probably have gotten little accomplished staying among this ritzy crowd of tourists with the enormous pool. Rafael explained that he was very close to his uncle and that his uncle insisted on him staying at the best place. His room was a suite arrangement and I could see that we would be comfortable for the night. We lounged around the pool area for a long time and then I excused myself from Rafael and went up to the room to go to bed early. The pullout couch was sufficient enough for me to doze off early. For some reason, I was beat.

I didn't hear Rafael come in but assumed he was in the bedroom when I woke up. I managed to make some coffee and was relaxing on the balcony when he shuffled out. We exchanged slow good mornings to each other. Just after that, my little cell phone rang. It was the Chief.

"Good morning, my friend, I am here with Inspector LaRacquet and we have some news that may be of some interest to you."

"Good morning, Chief. What's happening?"

"Well, it appears that your friend with the bulging eyes has been done in."

"Done in? . . . You mean killed?"

"Yes, very much so. He was a guest at the hotel on the opposite end of the beach as to where you stay. He was discovered by a maid in his room. We are at a loss as to who may have placed the bullet in his forehead and are certain that it is not in relation to the activities for which Inspector LaRacquet is our guest."

"Wow," I said in disbelief. It seemed things were heating up.

"What is it, Dean?" Rafael was whispering off to the side.

I pulled the phone away and told Rafael that Lt. Roger had been shot and killed.

The Chief continued. "We know that you and Rafael were together and that you had no involvement with this dreadful act and we know that this is not in relation to Inspector LaRacquet's business, so it appears that we may have what you would call a loose cannon in our presence and a dangerous one at that."

"I guess so, man; he was military, you know. Navy. Did you notify the military?"

"We have not—as soon as we got this news we wanted to notify you so the necessary precautions can be taken by you. We will be in touch with United States personnel immediately."

"Yes." I was still kind of dazed. "He was stationed at the Jacksonville, Florida base."

I felt bad for Lt. Roger. Not that I really cared that much for him. From what I knew, he wasn't very likeable.

Rafael wanted details but I didn't have much to give. Just a shot in the forehead in his hotel room and that it was not Inspector LaRacquet–related. Rafael thought he knew what hotel it may have been.

I thought about asking Rafael about Inspector LaRacquet's business here, but I didn't really feel it was related to my situation. I thought if the Chief or Inspector LaRacquet thought I should know something, they would let me know. Right now, I was concerned with something that was serious enough to get a U.S. military officer killed. I was beginning to understand why Jaime had appeared so nervous and anxious to get away from me. Up until now this whole thing had had sort of a comic effect to it, with Ralph and the blockmen. This whole thing was about me chasing Jaime for Marcia, not about the money. At least from my perspective. I had never cared about the money, it wasn't even an afterthought. Maybe my obsession with Marcia had clouded my ability to recognize that money, in this picture, was the most important thing to everyone but Marcia and me. Apparently, money drove Jaime to do what he did, money drove Whitey to dispatch Ralph and the blockmen, money is why Lt. Roger confronted us and now money must be why Lt. Roger had an extra hole in his head. Money. How much money? What had Jaime gotten into? All of a sudden this thing had gotten very serious.

Rafael answered his phone and spoke rapid Spanish. I could tell it was the Chief and that the conversation was dramatic.

When he hung up he said, "My uncle wants us to return to Santiago; he fears for our safety here."

I felt like a little kid. "But I haven't really talked with Jaime," I pleaded.

"Dean, my uncle does not become alarmed easily and he appears to be alarmed. Murder is not a common thing here."

"Listen, how long do you have this room here?"

"Until I choose to leave. One of the benefits of being associated with the police is that we may use this room for as long as we wish."

"OK, you go back and let me stay here. No one knows that I am here and, besides that, I am not in danger. No one wants anything from me. Hell, I don't even know what is wanted from who. So you go back, I'll talk to Jaime and then I will let you know when I am ready."

I felt fairly confident that Rafael would not pursue how it was that Jaime and I were going to hook up.

"But Dean, my uncle will kill me if I do not return with you."

"It's fine, I'll just hang out here, talk to Jaime, and then get a hold of you. If you don't mind coming back to get me."

"When do you plan on returning to Santiago?"

"I really don't want to stay beyond tomorrow. I told Jaime that I was not staying."

"OK, we stay together and I will deal with my uncle. It does not make sense for me to leave today, without you, only to return tomorrow. But I know that if Lt. Roger's killer is not caught today then my uncle will insist we return tomorrow."

"Fair enough."

We reached an agreement. It wasn't the best but I could live with it. I just had to figure out how I was going to ditch Rafael so that I could go back to the area of my old place and hope that Jaime would show up.

We went down to the buffet and ate a huge breakfast. I snagged a couple of matchbooks to be certain I knew of this resort's name, and we headed out to the pool area.

"Is this Jaime guy supposed to call you?"

"Yes," I lied as we lay down in some lounge chairs. Rafael had dressed appropriately in a surfer-type swimsuit while I had my usual jeans, sandals, and t-shirt. I pulled a big shade umbrella over. It wasn't long before Rafael was asleep on his chair and I was able to quietly but quickly sneak away from him and head down the big stone staircase to the beach.

As I walked quickly in the direction of my old room, I was careful not to pass too closely, but I could still see that the window had not been replaced and there was police tape forming a big X over the area of the window. I could not think of anywhere to go so I hung out in the area of the overturned boat where I had last seen Jaime. I didn't notice anyone unusual in that area. I hadn't been there that long, I had just started on my first Onyx of the day when Dan/Jim appeared at my chairside.

"Dean, that guy in your picture came in asking for you a couple of hours ago. He said if we see you that we should tell you Jaime was looking for you and that you should leave a message as to how he should get a hold of you. He is going to call our place around six tonight."

"Hmm, so he isn't coming back here?"

"No, man, he was nervous, it seemed like, looking around a lot. I asked him if he wanted to leave his number and he said you could leave your contact information for him. Said he wanted to see you in person."

"OK, err. . . ." I didn't know if this was Jim or Dan. "Well, thanks."

I thought for a second. "I'm staying at the . . . well, here." It occurred to me I had the matchbooks so I reached in my pocket, pulled one out, and gave it to him.

"I'm in room 610; you have something we can write that on there with?"

"No, no pen on me, but I'll remember . . . room 610."

"Yes, great. I will wait for him there and I know it will be sometime after 6:00. Thanks a lot, and if I don't see you again, good luck to you guys here; you've got a great place."

"Thanks, man. I'll tell Dan. Stop in next time. We've got that sissy beer for you."

I laughed. "OK, take care, Jim."

CHAPTER TWENTY-SIX

headed back, a long, slow, Onyx-puffing walk down the beach. I was confident that no one was following me and confident that I would see Jaime this evening. The initial shock of Lt. Roger being shot had apparently worn off, because although I couldn't explain why he had been killed, now it seemed less related to Jaime. Perhaps he was killed by a person trying to rob him. I knew the connection was there. Jaime being here in the DR, me visiting Lt. Roger, me going to the DR, Lt. Roger showing up in the DR—all was very interrelated but for some reason I didn't feel as though I was in danger. If it was related, maybe the killer was just on one mission, to kill Lt. Roger, and having done so he was on his merry way. Probably not merry way. I can't imagine someone who could put a bullet in someone else's forehead as being on their merry way.

Rafael was mad at me when I got back. I was in trouble because I hadn't answered his repeated calls to my little cell phone as I peacefully strolled the beach on my return. He had been about ready to call his uncle on me.

I was truthful with him and told him that I expected Jaime to show up to our room any time after 6:00 p.m. Then I went up to the room to change into my swimsuit so that I could enjoy the rest of the day lying around the pool.

It was an enjoyable day. I felt as though I was on a vacation at this resort. Rafael talked with several young blonde girls who seemed to be on vacation with their family, and I occasionally dipped into the pool to get wet before taking my place back in the lounge chair. I drank fruit drinks, ate a plate of fruit, and smoked a cigar (to which no one objected).

Rafael asked me if it was OK that he tell his uncle that we were expecting Jaime after the six o'clock hour. I said sure. I really liked Rafael; he was a good, honest kid, and we discussed his plans to enroll in college in the U.S. I told him, honestly, that if he needed help and I could provide it, then I would. Things seemed right with the world. Not for Lt. Roger, of course, but for those of us around this pool.

I was going to meet with Jaime. Get his version of what was going on in his life and what his intentions were with Marcia. I was anticipating that my mission would be accomplished. I could head back to the Turtle and resume my life either with or without Marcia. I was ready to be back to that routine, that not-a-care peacefulness. This chasing around was exciting in the very beginning but now it was taking on the feel of detective work again. I was over that. So I guess this was a nice experiment in reviving whatever lingering detective desires that remained and then squishing those desires to return to the new life I had chosen. I was ready to get this meeting over with and move on. The big question would be the money. What was this money that Whitcy and the late Lt. wanted? The Marcia thing was going to be easy. Either she was in his future or she was not. Maybe I would find out about this money and be able to let Ralph and his henchmen know.

I dozed off again. The sun off to an angle, the breeze coming in from the ocean, and the calypso music of the poolside band had made this too relaxing.

"Dean, Dean. It is nearly 6:00 p.m."

It was Rafael gently waking me up. I was a bit dazed but managed to say, "OK, I am going to head up. You can stay here if you want."

"No, I would like to go with you, if you do not mind."

"No, of course not. You can meet Jaime. I have a feeling if he is staying in this country then he may need some friends here."

We headed to the elevator and back to our room.

I changed out of my swimsuit in the bathroom and got into my usual clothes.

Rafael changed and we waited. And waited. I was sitting on the balcony looking out at the fading sun over the ocean when there was a solid knock on the door.

I told Rafael, who was watching some Spanish-speaking soap opera and lying on the couch, that I would get the door.

I went to the door and looked out the peek hole. It was Jaime all right, looking like he was in a fishbowl through the peek hole.

I opened the door.

"Jaime," I said. My smile was short lived. He was ushered through the door by a tall thin man wearing sunglasses who had a gun to Jaime's back.

"Back up," the man said in a stern, disturbingly calm voice. He was as tall as me but very thin and taut. He had a lightweight suit on, a worn gray in color, and his tie was thin and light blue. He locked the door behind him and moved inward into the suite.

I slowly took a couple steps back but Rafael was like a small attacking fearless terrier. He immediately and quickly moved toward the man, saying, "Hey, what the hell?"

The man casually slid around Jaime, gun still in hand, and as soon as Rafael was within his long reach, hit Rafael in the forehead with a quick burst of his arm. It happened so fast; Rafael was hit and immediately flew back across the floor. He was out cold and blood was seeping from his forehead. I instinctively moved to help him. The calm voice returned with "Hold it," and the gun was leveled at my head. I held up. It was clear that Rafael was out. I was worried for him and my attention turned to the thin man. I wanted revenge. I felt like a father wanting to protect his son. Jaime was shaking, and I felt disgust for him.

"Sit down," the man said as he pointed his gun to a chair at the table while holding on to Jaime. I was a few feet from

Rafael when I sat in the chair and could hear his breathing and some low, slow moans. I thought he was going to be OK, so my focus was on the thin man. He was hard. His face, behind those sunglasses, was the one I saw at my old hotel room. He had been watching me then. I was certain his gun was the one that had killed Lt. Roger. His gun had a silencer on it. This was not a good sign. I had only seen a silencer on guns a couple of times throughout my whole police career and each time it was not good. It occurred to me that Jaime had good reason to be shaking.

"Let's talk" was the command.

"OK, that's fine by me."

"This will go much easier if you tell me up front where the money is."

"And, if I don't know where the money is?"

"Then I start by putting a bullet in that grease spot on the floor" and he pointed the gun at Rafael.

My heart raced. I stood. Not quickly or aggressively but I stood. I placed myself between the gun and Rafael. The thin man didn't make me sit down, didn't yell. Just smiled. An evil crack in the marble face of a smile. Like a serpent almost. I did not like this situation at all.

"There are three of you. I can place bullets in the most painful of areas without killing you. One of you will eventually speak. One of you will tell me where the money is before it is all over."

I wanted to get closer to him. I knew from a distance he had the advantage. I started taking slow steps to him saying, "Let's just talk. . . ." I was moving extremely slow, almost motionless, hoping he would let me continue to close the distance. He was about to say something, his serpent mouth was opening, when, bam, the door of the room came blasting off its hinges, splintering and crunching. I didn't know what was happening to the door, I just sprang forward, focused on the gun. He was quick but I followed the angle of his arm as he tried to raise the gun up and out of my reach. I was able to grab his arm above the elbow and I squeezed his arm as hard as I could while pushing him back. The gun went off but I could barely hear it. I was aware of police officers flooding through the door and I was able to plow the thin man into the oncoming officers. They absorbed him and violently subdued him. Jaime was cowering off in a corner in almost a fetal position. Stepping through the remaining wood on the door was Inspector LaRacquet.

"Inspector La Tennis Racquet, man, am I glad to see you," and I meant it.

Right behind him was Chief Aquino. The sight of the Chief immediately turned my thoughts to Rafael. I turned and got to Rafael's side quickly. He was moaning and seemed to be sort of coming around. The Chief rushed over.

"Did that man do this to my nephew?"

I just nodded my head yes.

The Chief turned and went to where two officers were finishing putting the cuffs on the thin man and administered a case of police brutality. The thin man and his dangerous gun were dragged away by the officers. Medical personnel arrived and took care of Rafael. They assured us, as best they could, that he would be all right but that he had probably suffered a concussion. They took him out on a stretcher; he was somewhat awake when he was being wheeled out. The four of us—Inspector LaRacquet, the Chief, Jaime, and I— all sat down around the table. The Chief spoke. And as he spoke, he pointed a finger directly at Jaime. Jaime was still shaking.

"I do not know who you are or why you are here. That is not my concern. But, because of you, my nephew suffers in pain. I am ordering you out of this country. I will give you all of tomorrow to make arrangements. Should you be here the day after tomorrow, you will be arrested and experience the painfully slow process of our legal system. Have I made myself clear?"

"Yessir," Jaime managed.

Then the Chief turned to me.

"My friend, let us talk in the privacy of the hallway."

I got up with the Chief and the Inspector and the three of us headed to the hallway while Jaime sat dejectedly at the table.

When we got to the hallway, after making sure no one was around, the Chief in a low voice told me that the person that they just arrested, the thin man, was suspected of working for a very secretive branch of the U.S. government. That this branch either in whole or in part had actually broken away from the government. It had run amok and was rumored to be in need of funding. That this branch of the government did things the public was not aware of and often engaged in very sinister activity. While not the CIA, it had been a branch that engaged heavily in drug activities. The Chief did not know why this thin man was interested in Jaime but that Jaime must have been involved in something very serious. The Chief assured me that I would no longer have a problem from this particular man but that I needed to find out what Jaime was involved in, and if it concerned him, his department, or his country, I would need to inform him. I assured him I would. He emphasized that he trusted my judgment. Chief Aquino was a strong, forceful man who was able to take control of situations. The kind of man you want on your side.

"What will happen to the guy?" I asked.

"As I have told you, my friend, Inspector LaRacquet is here because we have knowledge of a massive Haitian-Colombian drug smuggling operation that will pass through our jurisdiction any day now. This will be a massive transport of drugs headed to France. We have been working on the investigation for several years. The man who hurt my nephew will be caught in this drug bust. He will not be able to be identified and will be in the system a very, very long time with many Haitian and Colombians. Once he is identified, if he is, he will be charged with the murder of a U.S. military officer. This man may never see the light of day again."

Inspector LaRacquet nodded his approval.

"Now, go and learn what you must from your friend inside. I did not mean to be too harsh on him but I see no good in his remaining in this country. We are a police force with few resources, we have invested much in preventing this drug operation and are near the end of finances for our department, and we cannot afford to protect him any longer."

"How did you know, Chief? That the thin man was coming here?"

"We located your Jaime immediately before my nephew placed the call to me informing me that Jaime was to appear here. Then we became aware that this 'thin man,' as you call him, was following Jaime. It did not feel as a right situation to us, so we thought we would follow along."

"Well, thank God you did."

I shook their hands and headed back into the suite to talk with Jaime. He was still visibly shaken.

CHAPTER TWENTY-SEVEN

"Jesus, Dean, what I have done? What have I gotten into?"

"Lt. Roger is dead."

This didn't calm him down any but I wanted to catch him off guard, to see if he knew him and what his reaction would be.

"What? God damn."

It appeared he was trying to process it.

"Where? When? How?"

"Well, I think he came here looking for you."

"Wait a minute . . . wait a minute . . . how did you know Lt. Roger? How did you know about us?"

"About you, what about you? What about you and Lt. Roger? Tell me everything, Jaime, I need to know, and for your own safety, you better tell me."

"Aw man." He had both elbows on the table and was rubbing his head with both hands. Hotel repair guys were starting to show up.

"Let's get outta here," I said. "We'll take a walk and you can tell me everything."

I did this as much to get us outside so I could light one up as much as to avoid the distraction of the hotel repair guys.

We didn't talk on the way down, but as soon as we hit the cement surrounding the pool he asked, "You think Marcia would take me back, Dean? I just know that I want to get back to her, with her."

He pleadingly asked me this just as I discovered all three of the Onyxs that were in my pocket were broken, all nearly in half. I should have had them in a protective case, but then again, I hadn't thought I'd be getting into a struggle with a thin reptilian man. So Jaime's expression of desire to get back with Marcia and me trying to light a smashed-up Onyx really put a damper on my mood. I wanted to hear him say something to the effect that he loved this island

and wanted to stay and become king of the sanky pankies and ask me to clear things up with the Chief so that could happen. Instead he was one step away from asking me to take on the role of Cupid.

"Listen Jaime, we can deal with that later. Lt. Roger was murdered. We were in some serious shit up in that room and now I gotta figure out if there are any more people out there who may be dangerous." I was losing patience.

"OK, man, OK."

I got the cigar lit by the time we were down the stone stairs and walking on the sand. I looked around but it didn't seem like there was anyone around that posed a threat.

So we talked.

"Man, Dean, this is so deep. I'm gonna tell you some shit that very few people know about. Crazy how I got all mixed up in it but, I did. You remember back at the end of the war in Iraq?"

"Yeah, sure."

"Well, if you remember, there was a big deal about missing money that the government was secretly sending to Iraq, cash . . . cash bundled up in packets of one hundred dollar bills and sent over on C-140s."

"C-140s?"

"Yeah, man, C-140s, planes. . . . So, the government was afraid that Iraq would be all unstable and shit after the war and they wanted to get cash over there and get it spread around. Only someone thiefed a ton of it. Something like six billion. Six billion, man. Six billion dollars just lost, stolen, whatever. So, the fucking U.S. government secretly flies a ton of U.S. cash over to Iraq, only to lose it or have it stolen."

"Six billion? That was the amount?" I was struggling with keeping my poor excuse of a cigar going as we were slowly, casually walking in the cool sand of the evening beach.

"Yeah, probably more, some reports are it may have been up to twelve billion. Anyway, the government came out years later and supposedly found the money. Yeah, right. Well, after this happened and after the public found out, the government had to stop with this secret money shit."

"I would think so."

"Ha, well not for long. Turns out the American attention span is not that great, different president but same shit, same government. So they started up again. But since Iraq isn't the big deal it was back then, not so much money and certainly not all at once. Kind of like our government is keeping them on a very small allowance, just enough to pay off certain informants and officials. But the American public wouldn't understand so it has to be kept a secret."

He was surprising me with his inside knowledge and the way he was talking.

"How do you know this?"

"I'm involved, Dean. I'm in this shit." He spread his arm out like the whole beach was the problem. Like the whole beach was "this shit." He seemed to be getting all nervous again.

"Dean, I gotta get out of this. Will she take me back?" he pleaded.

"Yes, she'll take you back." He was desperate and I couldn't lie. I knew she would take him back.

"You gotta get me out of this, I can't live like this. You were a detective. You know how to get outta shit like this. You gotta take charge, man. I'll do whatever you want. Just get me out of it."

Oh, so now I was a detective but when he talked to Marcia about me I was some sort of mall security guy. But I was feeling sorry for him in a way. He was almost crying.

"OK, but I need to know everything."

Everything turned out to be a lot and it took a long time to explain. We walked far down the beach and turned around and walked back slowly and I spent a lot of time trying to light another poor broken cigar.

So this was it: Jaime, who was working for Whitey, was instructed to meet Lt. Roger in a bar one night. Lt. Roger wasn't friendly to Jaime but he explained that he was somehow associated with Whitey. Jaime never did come to know how, as Lt. Roger never wanted to disclose that and Jaime figured he didn't need to know anyway.

Lt. Roger was the Navy pilot in charge of some secret flights in the middle of the night from the base in Jacksonville to Iraq; it was his and Whitey's plan that he would drop a very large bundle off the coast, in the Florida Keys. Jaime would be provided the exact coordinates. Jaime was to retrieve this bundle in his seaplane and take it back to Whitey. Jaime did as he was told. The first, second, and third times he did this, it was nearly flawless. The bundle was exactly where Lt. Roger always said it would be. The bundles were big and heavy. Each bundle was a bundle of cash.

Jaime got to know Lt. Roger. Jaime never really like Lt. Roger but they often had drinks together when Lt. Roger would come to Miami. Jaime had learned that the U.S. government was still supplying Iraq with cash. Not as much and as often as before, but they still were. Lt. Roger was in total control of this transport and he had figured out that once he dropped it at the designated spot in Iraq, the Iraqis retrieved it. No accountability to the United States. Chop a little off the bundle, bundle that up, and drop it off the plane in the Keys, just like he did in Iraq, and no one would know the difference. Only this bundle would be smaller, and Whitey would be responsible for retrieving it, with Lt. Roger getting his cut. So what if the Iraqis got stiffed a little?

Enter Jaime. Whitey's man with the perfect plane for the job. Jaime did it several times and got paid a little extra for his trouble. He never did know what the split was between Whitey and Lt. Roger. But Jaime wanted a drastic lifestyle change. He was tired of Miami. Jaime thought a lot. Thought of his lifestyle, thought of how dangerous Whitey might be, and thought of Marcia. He and Marcia's life together had become boring. The sex the same each time and he knew they were both unhappy. Jaime was tired. Tired of the same old. What's a man without dreams and ambition? So, Jaime thought, what if he picked up the bundle and kept going? He could fly to the DR, a place he loved, and live off the millions he had. He'd get in shape, lose the gut he had let himself gain and enjoy life. He never knew how much exactly was in each bundle but he knew he could live like a king in the DR. He had been to the DR. He knew he could live like a king. Maybe they would think his plane had crashed. Even if they didn't, they would not find him in the DR. So, when Lt. Roger gave him the dates and the coordinates, he was ready. He was hoping it was a smaller bundle. He didn't need a ton and perhaps they would forget about it even if they didn't think he had crashed.

Jaime's problem, his only concern, was Marcia. Well, Marcia and whether or not Whitey was going to come after him. He could not tell her anything. He had to just do it. He convinced himself that he didn't love her that much anymore. Sure, they had been through a lot together, but maybe they needed a break. After time, if he missed her and all was forgotten by Whitey, and he had grown tired of sanky pankies, he could figure out how to get her to the DR.

He was ready. He was confident. He didn't pack anything and didn't say any different type of goodbye to anyone and he headed out. The bundle was where Lt. Roger had told him it was. He got it loaded and instead of turning back to the mainland like he usually did, he headed to the coast off of Santiago. He could land in the water there and begin his island life.

What he didn't count on was his nervous paranoia. From the moment he landed, he was nervous and paranoid. He had a plane parked in the sea off the coast of Santiago with $10 million of stolen U.S. cash aboard it.

"Ten million?" I gasped and almost swallowed my poor excuse of a cigar.

It was $10 million. He figured that Lt. Roger was dropping around $100 million and that he had shaved off and bundled $10 million.

"Ten million?"

"Yeah, man, ten million dollars on my plane. Sittin' out there." He pointed to the ocean.

"Wait, wait, ten million dollars?"

"Yeah. What was I thinking? What the hell did I think I was going to do? And, it turns out, I miss Marcia like crazy, man. You gotta find a way out. Am I in too deep, Dean?"

I immediately wondered if I was in too deep. A U.S. military officer had been murdered. Apparently, the thin man was some sort of hitman that was connected to some crazy-assed branch, or ex-branch, of the government, and even Whitey, whoever the hell he is, was after this money. This wasn't just a self-imposed mission to find Jaime; this was some serious shit.

"Jesus, Jaime. Ten million dollars? What does ten million dollars even look like? How big is it?" I didn't know if this could fit in several briefcases or if it took up his whole plane. I seriously had no idea. He could have told me anything. Was he sitting on stacks of bills while he was flying?

"There are ten stacks, each stack is a little higher than a yardstick. It's big but not as big as you would think. It's all one hundred dollar bills."

"Man." I was in shock. So this is what all the "where's the money?" had been about.

"So Jaime, if all had gone as they planned, Whitey would have gotten the ten million and then paid you, Lt. Roger, and whoever else."

"Yes, that would be it. We did it before. I don't know if it was 10 or not, I never opened the bundles till this one."

I was wondering how the thin man had known about the money and Jaime missing. What made him, them, interested in this bundle? Why didn't they send a thin man after the others? Is this the only one they knew about? Did they find out about the others and then decided to try to track this one down? Probably. Sounded like that would be Jaime's luck. I could only think that Lt. Roger had either willingly or not so willingly let him or them know about it.

"Can you help me, man? This isn't worth it. I'm not big time."

"Yes," I instinctively said and regretted it right away.

"How? What do we do?"

"Can you take me to the money?"

"Sure, we can go now."

He had rented a boat. A little fishing boat to get back and forth to the plane. It was tied up back down the beach. By the time we had finished our talk, we were nearly back at the hotel. We went up to the room Rafael had rented. The door was nearly fixed. I was really wanting to find out about Rafael but my mind was occupied with what we should do.

CHAPTER TWENTY-EIGHT

We left the hotel again. I was beginning to get tired of this walk but we did it anyway. The same walk down the beach toward my old room. We didn't say much. Jaime was pleading some more but I didn't really hear him. I was thinking. My mind was racing. I looked around often. I didn't want any more thin men popping up. I was getting nervous. I could understand how Jaime felt. His nervousness.

We walked past my old room and the window was still out, the tape still there. I guess the rate of repair was one of the big differences between a local place and a touristy place. Not much farther down the beach we reached a marina. Well, not really a marina but a place where there were boats docked on two long piers. The strong ocean breeze was causing the boats to slap against the piers and each other. It had become another cloudless, beautiful night. There were stars and a bright moon as we walked down the first pier to where Jaime stopped at a small fishing boat. He jumped down into it with little problem and I managed to get in also without tipping us. He got the pull-start motor going and we were off. I sat on the front bench while Jaime took a big wide turn to take us down the beach right past where we had walked. The breeze picked up as we increased our speed and the ocean mist hit me each time we bounced off a wave. I watched the lights of the Cabarete. I could hear the muffled sound of voices and music. People were enjoying themselves. I should be enjoying myself. I should be here, with Marcia, enjoying a romantic getaway. But I knew I had to give up on Marcia. I would get Jaime back to her. Maybe she would hate him and be done with him. I didn't know.

We flew past the resort area, less lights now. No music and voices. It was quiet, moonlit, and beautiful. Jaime called my name and I looked back to see him pointing at an area. The area of the ocean had anchored boats, some yachts. It was like a little village of swaying boats. Lit up and peaceful-looking.

We slowed way down and took a wide turn around a yacht, and then I saw the plane. Anchored and swaying like the boats. It wasn't the only plane but it looked to be the nicest. There appeared to be five other planes anchored there. The planes looked so different, but they added an element to this village of boats. It looked cool. Jaime's plane was bigger than I had expected and, as we got close, I could see the Pitt colors. The blue and gold.

Pulling alongside one of the rudders, Jaime expertly tied the boat tight against it. We balanced ourselves getting out and standing on the rudder. I think they were called rudders. The plane was extremely well balanced; it hardly tilted with both of us on the one side. Maybe it was the weight of one hundred dollar bills the size of a mattress stacked inside the plane evening it out. Jaime punched some numbers on a key pad and a door underneath the plane opened up and he pulled some steps out. We climbed in. It was roomy but would have been much roomier if the bundle hadn't been in there. It looked imposing enough, realizing it was all money. I went over and felt it. Hard, like bricks. It was still tightly wrapped, in some sort of waterproof substance, but I could feel the division of rows. Five rows of two and, yes, it was taller than a yardstick.

"Have you used any of it?"

"No, I've been too afraid. I know it's not marked. The last thing the government wants is one hundred million dollars being traced back, but I just couldn't bring myself to spend it. Besides, I had enough money to get by."

"So, this is ten million?"

"Yep, this is it."

I thought I had developed a plan and the sight of this hadn't changed it. I didn't think this was unmanageable.

"Jaime, you've been begging me to get you out of this. To take over. You still want that to happen?"

The moon had been providing light through the small windows but Jaime flipped a switch and small lights lit up the interior. He looked up at me.

"Yeah, Dean, that's it. I need you to take over. I really don't care about the money anymore."

"OK, can you fly this thing back to the U.S. without getting noticed? Back to Miami?"

Jaime had pulled a bottle of whiskey or scotch or something out of a cabinet and took a swig and then handed it to me.

"No, I'm good, and you need to stop, you need to rest. Can you sleep on this thing and take off first thing in the morning?"

"Sure, I'd love to get back to Miami, but what about everyone wanting the money?"

"Well, I know for certain the thin man isn't going to be bothering us. Lt. Roger is dead. You think he had anyone working with him?"

"No, man, no one who would know about me."

"OK, then we should be good."

"Whitey—Dean, you're forgetting about Whitey. It's his money. Well, the government's really, but he stole it, fair and square. He'll kill me, man."

"No, he won't."

"Dean, you don't know Whitey—do you know Whitey? Dean, you don't know Whitey, do you?" The desperation was coming back in. He was afraid.

"No, I don't, but I know guys like him. We'll have to deal with him."

"We're gonna have to, Dean, he's not going to let ten million dollars go."

"OK, let's stop. We have to get organized here."

"OK, Dean, tell me what to do." He was trying to calm himself down.

"I'm going to take the boat and head back to the beach. You're going to stay here and take off in the morning. I'm going to take a flight back to Miami and we are going to meet up there. You got another place to dock this thing other than the one you use when you normally take the money back to the Miami?"

"Yes, I really do. I can call my guy when I am in flight tomorrow and he'll let me right in."

"Does Whitey know about this other place?"

"No, I've never used it. Friend of mine keeps offering for me to use it but I pay for the one I have in Miami."

"All right, now listen. That's the only call you make. No calling Marcia. When you land you call my bar. You have something I can write the number on?"

He looked around and ended up handing me a flight log–looking thing and a pen. I wrote down the number for the Turtle.

"So, when you land, call my bar right away and tell whoever answers that you have landed. Give me your number, write your number down but also give it when you call the bar in case I lose it. I'll call you right after you call my bar. I don't have a cell phone."

"OK." He wrote it down and gave it to me. I put the number in my pocket.

"I'm going to take the boat, head back, but I am also taking half of one of those stacks. Five hundred thousand dollars. We are going to invest in some protection."

I think he started to balk. I was thinking maybe his "I really don't care about the money anymore" had lost its sincerity or maybe he thought I was going to simply take off with part of his money. But he didn't question it. He got a big knife out and started cutting the wrapping. He was able to count out half a row pretty quickly. He even had a large duffle bag that we were able to put the cash in. I threw it down into the boat.

I climbed down into the boat.

"Listen, Jaime, do exactly what I told you and don't touch that money."

I got the boat going and sped off into the moonlit night. When I got some distance away, I slowed the boat down to neutral and floated. I got out the small flip phone and dialed the Chief.

"Chief?"

"My friend Dean, it is late, this is not like you; is all well?"

"Yes, how is Rafael?"

"Aw, he is fine. His headache is very large but he is resting. I believe him to be quite fond of one of the nurses."

"Oh, great. That's really good. Listen, Chief, I was wondering if someone could pick me up at the hotel where Rafael was staying, out front, and if I could come to your office?"

"Surely, my friend. What time would you like for one of my officers to be there?"

"In about an hour would be perfect, Chief, thanks."

We hung up and after docking the boat in the same dock space and lugging two bags down the beach to the front of the hotel, I was picked up by an officer in a marked police car. We rode, pretty much in silence, back to the police department.

CHAPTER TWENTY-NINE

It was late and I was wondering if I had kept the Chief up and around his office but, if so, he sure didn't seem upset about it. He greeted me in his office with a big smile, supplied me with a couple cigars, and offered me a seat.

"Chief, I am leaving tonight. Jaime will be leaving as well. But, before I go, I wanted to provide some help in your fight against crime here. So here is some money."

I carried the bag around his desk to where he was sitting. I plopped it down and he opened it. He was shocked.

"My friend, what is it you have given me?"

"Well, it isn't mine personally, Chief, but it is five hundred thousand dollars. The U.S. government was trying to give it away and it ended up here. That's about all I can say. It's not traceable and it would be much better used here, in your fight to keep this island great, than where the government wanted to send it. I only ask one thing."

"Of course, of course." The Chief was visible thrilled and I found it somewhat disconcerting that he was so accepting. I guess no questions asked. It occurred to me that he had probably been in similar situations before. Probably not much red tape in his job.

"Hopefully, the thin man. The guy that hit Rafael. Hopefully he was the only one. If he gets out or if there are others, I need for them to somehow think all the money is gone. That Jaime, although he did have it, does not now and that I don't have it. We can't be looking back over our shoulders after this. You think you can help me out with that?"

"I can devise such a plan. I can provide rumors and reports of how very much money came to no longer be in your friend's possession. My friend, I would have done this for you without this amazing gift to our police department, I can assure you, my friend, this money will be money I can use to make my department better."

I stood and extended my hand.

"Chief, I am glad I got to know you. I wish you the best and I hope Rafael gets up and about soon."

He grabbed my hand and pulled me into a big hug.

"My friend." He slapped at my back.

"Hey, Chief, you think I can get a ride to the airport?"

I arrived at the airport and only had to wait forty-five minutes for the next flight to Miami. I was happy to be leaving. I loved the DR and vowed to return for a leisurely visit without having guns pointed at me. On the flight, I dozed very briefly, it seemed, but was awakened on our descent into the Miami airport. As soon as I was in the airport, I could feel the difference. I think I liked the laid-back casualness of the DR as opposed to the instant hustle and bustle that was so American, even at this early morning hour. Anyway, I didn't feel as though I had time to dwell. I guess I was submerged into the hustle and bustle already.

I took a cab to the nearest hotel. Got partially undressed and lay down for a nap. There wasn't much I could do at this early morning hour. When I woke it was past eight and the Miami sun was shining through the dusty windows. I felt like I had overslept but there was no one to talk to about it. After a very fast shower, I went downstairs and got a cab back to the airport. All this time, from the moment I got to the airport in the DR, I had been checking to see if it looked like anyone was following me.

I got to the airport and found the car rental booth and rented a Honda minivan. I thought that would be pretty nondescript while being able to hold a load of things. I got it one way to Jacksonville. I asked the girl at the rental counter if I could use the phone, and she allowed me. I called the Turtle, taking a chance that it would be open this early.

"Sandy Turtle, may I help you?"

"Hey, Rose, it's Dean."

"Dean, I don't be knowing no Dean. Used to know one that worked here. Well, he never really worked here. Would show up once in a while. Then, one day, this skinny little woman showed up and I haven't seen that Dean since," and she hung up the phone.

I looked at the girl behind the counter. She didn't care, so I called again.

I heard "Sandy Turtle" in a singing Dean Martin–like tone.

"Jerry?"

"Oh, hey, Dean. Rosie here says that she isn't here," followed by a chuckle and then he whispered into the phone, "Listen Dean, I'm coming right at you to tell you that I am circumventing you to work this out between you and Rose."

"What? Jerry, give me Rose," I said maybe a bit too sternly. I heard the phone being handed.

"What you want?"

"Rose, listen, I'll be back very soon. I am sorry that I didn't contact you when I was gone. I couldn't, really. Is everything OK?"

"You know damn well everything is fine here. I'll let you have a piece of my mind when you get your ass back here."

"OK, OK, cool. I will be back, maybe as soon as today. Has anyone called the place saying they have landed?"

"No, ain't no one called."

"OK, I'll be calling back, but if someone calls and said they landed, tell them I'll be in touch soon. Oh, and get their number just in case. I know the dude but get his number."

She could sense my seriousness. Of course she could. She was Rose, Rosie.

"Dean, you OK?"

"Rosie, I am fine," I said calmly. "I'll be back soon."

"You better."

I drove back to the hotel. I had not checked out and didn't have to check out until noon. I had some calls to make and didn't want to hog the girl's rental stand phone.

When I called the Turtle later, Rose finally informed me that Jaime had, in fact, called and she said she had a number. I wrote it down on the notepad but I knew it was the same one Jaime had given me. I had looked at that number more than once. So I called it.

"Hello."

"Jaime, it's me, Dean."

"Man, Dean, I'm glad to hear your voice. What are we doing? I'm fuckin freakin out flying all around with this onboard."

"Well, I'm going to come and pick you up now. Everything go OK?"

"Yeah, man, sure. Other than me being freaked, I just flew in, found the dock. Didn't sleep last night but I made it man."

"OK, give me the address, and don't let the plane out of your sight."

"I'm looking at it right now."

"OK, give me the address. I need to make a couple stops but I'll be there soon."

He gave me the address. I wrote it down and then I went to my bag and got yet another number out of my bag and dialed that number.

"This is Rafael."

It wasn't Rafael. Rafael was back in the DR with an ice pack on his head trying to get a nurse to go out with him. This was Ralph.

"Hey, Ralph, it's Dean. Hunter"

"Dean, what the hell? Chew with Jaime?"

"No, but I need to see Whitey today."

"What, what chew talkin' about?"

Being around Dominicans who spoke broken English, I was hoping there would come a time I could sit down with Ralph and tell him he needs to work on words other than "you" to pronounce in broken English if he was going to really pull this accent thing off.

"Listen, Ralph, it is very important that I meet with Whitey. This is about Jaime. He is going to want to hear what I have to say if he is still interested in Jaime."

"OK, OK, hold on, Dean. Let me talk to Whitey. He's a busy man, Dean."

"Well, just see if he's interested in Jaime and let me know. I don't have much time and I don't have a cell so get back to me right away, Ralph. Right away, Ralph. I'm gonna give you my number now, Ralph."

I was calling down to the front desk when Ralph called back. I was getting the location of a Dick's Sporting Goods store nearby. I quickly hung up to take Ralph's call.

"Dean, this better not be no monkey business. Whitey is not real happy right now with Jaime. This is not looking good for Jaime."

"I know, I know."

"Whitey's got guys out looking for him."

"All right, where am I meeting him and when?"

"Haha, where you meeting me, you mean. I'll take you to him. Seven p.m. at the Freedom Tower."

"OK," and I hung up. I knew what the Freedom Tower was but was not sure exactly how to get there. I'd worry about that later. Now I had to go to Dick's and get to where Jaime was waiting.

At Dick's I bought eight baseball equipment bags. All were the same, black and red.

CHAPTER THIRTY

The marina where I was to meet Jaime was beautiful. It took me a while to get there, but it was worth it. It was located near Virginia Key, sort of southeast of the city of Miami. It seemed as though there was nothing but different shades of blue ocean everywhere. There were a ton of boats, all kinds, and Jaime's seaplane was not the only one. There were several spread out throughout the docks. Bright white railings, bright blue ocean, and the bright colors of boats, jet skis, parasails. Did anyone work? People leisurely walking in their white sailing attire, clinking mixed drinks, while smiling and saying hello to one another. I vowed that back home I would get into the sailing crowd. Throw on some white clothing, grab a fake mixed drink, and walk around smiling and saying hello to everyone. But then again Fernandina Beach wasn't really your yacht club kind of crowd. Sure, we had the Plantation but for the most part we were a shrimpin' community. Tough sailor types. Those that sailed because they had to catch fish to make a living. Not those that sailed to impress friends or women half their age. My town was where jeans, a worn t-shirt, and a cigar fit right in. So, if I ever got done with this Jaime thing, I would return to walking around in jeans and my Pitt shirt, smoking a big ol' stogie, drinking a fake beer, smiling, and saying hello.

Jaime saw me first and flagged me down as I was walking down a lightweight metal ramp toward where the majority of boats were.

"Hey, Dean," he yelled, a bit too loud for my liking.

I looked around but didn't see anyone that appeared to be interested in us.

"Jaime, where's your plane?"

"Around the corner here, back up by where you came from. Isn't this place great? I've never been here, just been friends with the guy who manages it forever."

"Yes, it's great. Who all knows you are here?"

"Just him, the guy that runs the place."

"OK, money still on the plane?"

"Yes, I didn't touch it."

"OK, come to my car and help me get some things."

We went to the minivan. I threw Jaime three of the baseball bags and then picked up the remaining five. They were long equipment bags, designed to hold things like bats and catchers' equipment.

"What are we doing with this?"

"We're gonna put the money in these."

"OK, they got carts here if we are bringing it back to the van."

We went to the plane. It was hot inside but we did the work. We loaded each bag up, with two of the bags a little less full than the others. Jaime had gotten the cart and we wheeled the bags to my minivan. It appeared that no one was taking notice of us. I figure it was fairly common for people to be wheeling things to and from their yachts and near yachts. Common enough that they had carts for that doing that kind of thing. Plus, the way we were dressed we looked like we were lower on the social totem pole and probably workers wheeling things around. Kind of funny we happened to be wheelin' around millions of dollars. When we were done loading the van, I turned to Jaime. I threw him one of the bags that was different, much lighter. He, of course, dropped it, but picked it up right away. Man, this guy used to have some athletic ability, but not anymore.

He looked at me quizzically, while holding the bag. He looked like a sad little kid. Like I was throwing him his suitcase and saying, "Now, go on kid, get outta here."

"Jaime, there is five hundred thousand dollars in that bag. I want you to take it and go to Marcia. She wants you back. She is at her parents' house in Ohio. Take the money, go to her, and make a new life. But lay low. Realize what you have."

"Dean, I meant it when I said I didn't care about the money. I've had time to think. I know what is important."

"I know, but just take that. It will give you something to start over with."

"What about Whitey, man? I'm still freakin' out about him catching me, he does things to people."

"Don't worry about Whitey. I'll take care of him."

"OK, man, I'm gonna fly to Ohio now. Thank you, Dean, thank you so much. Be careful though—I'm tellin' ya, Whitey is a bad man."

We shook hands and it felt like we were old friends. We had been through a lot in the past days. We did have some history. Jesus, why was I even entertaining sentimental thoughts? This clown had stolen my one true love. Now, I was giving him $500,000, watching him climb into a cool plane to fly to Ohio to probably have monster make-up sex with the girl I loved, and here I was, left to confront the big, bad man Whitey.

CHAPTER THIRTY-ONE

As I was pulling out of the parking lot, I saw Jaime's plane taxiing past the row of boats headed out to the sea. I steered the minivan back toward the city. I found my way to the Miami Dade college area where the Freedom Tower was located. I was able to park on the street. I made sure it was in a spot that I was certain would not be towed. I was going to be leaving a minivan that had seven baseball equipment bags of cash in it, $9 million worth. I locked up the van and walked. I was starving. I couldn't really remember the last time I ate. I didn't feel like I had really taken advantage of the great food in the DR. I needed food now, and I needed a lot. I walked around for a while and then stumbled on a great place called Niu Kitchen that served Catalan food. It wasn't crowded and the menu seemed to fit my needs. I ordered a Beck's nonalcoholic beer, the Pa Amb Tomàquet, which was toasted bread, grated tomato, and garlic oil along with the Ous, which was poached eggs, truffled potato foam, ham, and black truffles. I ordered it without the ham, pounded it, and followed it with another Beck's, hoping it was not a last meal kind of thing. But while eating, I had experienced an amazing calmness far from the freakin' out that Jaime had been experiencing, not even bordering on nervousness.

The restaurant was only about a mile away from the Freedom Tower, and I used the time I had to walk the area. I needed movement. It had seemed like forever since I had exercised and my run with Rafael, from Lt. Roger, had left my leg muscles sore. Poor Lt. Roger. I felt bad for the coconut to the nose when he ended up with a bullet to the forehead. I often thought, what if you went in for a root canal, then immediately, upon leaving the dentist's parking lot, got in a car accident that killed you? Wouldn't that suck? Like Lt. Roger taking the coconut to the nose, hours before the bullet to the forehead.

The sun was making its move downward. It was getting close to seven. I strolled casually by the minivan just to make sure all was well. It appeared to be. I was certain, just based on the area, that it would be OK there even if this took hours. So I slowly walked to the Freedom Tower. Once there, I found my place against the low wall that extended the length of the front of the building.

The black Cadillac Escalade with very tinted windows was not hard to notice. It pulled up to the curb. I didn't move, just watched. The back window slid down and I could see Ralph's pudgy face smiling at me. I pushed myself away from the wall and slowly walked toward the vehicle. When I got close, the back door opened and I slid in. Through the freezing interior and an overwhelming cloud of men's cologne, I could see the blockmen sitting in the front seats. I couldn't remember which was which so, while shaking hands with Ralph, I said, "Nice to see you Ralph, gentlemen." I think they grunted in unison and Ralph said, "Nice to see chew as well, Dean. How's our mutual friend Jaime?"

The Cadillac eased away from the curb and out into the traffic.

"He's fine. Where we going?"

"We going to see Whitey and chew better have some good information for him, man."

"I do. Where's Whitey live?"

"Haha, you ain't goin' to Whitey's house, man. We takin' you to his business. His club, man."

"OK." I didn't feel like playing twenty questions with Ralph and just sank further into the leather of the overstuffed car seats. I must have gotten used to the smell because the only thing that bothered me was the temperature inside this thing. I noticed that all three of these jamokes were dressed in dark suits with ties. I closed my eyes and tried to enjoy the ride. I was sincerely hoping this was not the calm before the storm.

It didn't seem like we rode that long before we were there. Right on Ocean Drive in South Beach. There were people everywhere. It wasn't late enough for the night crowd. The sun was beginning to set and it was getting cooler but most of the people out were in their bathing suits, probably headed back to their swanky hotels to get ready to go out for the evening. The beautiful people, beautiful bodies coming off the beach, ready to turn into beautiful nightclub goers. They lived to be beautiful and to be around those that were beautiful. South Beach, baby, it doesn't get much more beautiful. Oh, how I longed for the quiet, star-filled easy nights of Fernandina Beach.

The SUV was directed into a vacant parking spot right on a corner. We were ushered in by a valet. The view from the backseat made it look like a plane pulling in after having landed. The valet slowly waved us into the spot and the one blockman expertly maneuvered the vehicle, while I watched through the lights of the interior and front window. I really was comfortable and didn't feel like getting out. But we did, all of us. We had business to do.

We left the SUV and all four of us went around the corner through the front door. I didn't see the name of the club because we were moving fast. I felt like some kind of famous guy or something. I was in my standard attire, left over from the DR; jeans, t-shirt, sandals. The three of them in their suits and me looking like the star who thought he didn't have to dress like everyone else when going to the club.

It was dark and thumping in the club. I could tell this was a place that would get packed as the night went on. It really was very nice. The four of us squeezed into an elevator that was tucked away in the right corner. Ralph had to use a key before the up button would work. I was thinking Ralph must have some authority with Whitey, which made me wonder about Whitey.

The blockmen and I alone would have had a hard time fitting in the elevator, so with Ralph we were smushed together.

"Ralph, what is Whitey's name?"

"Chew can just call him Whitey. He'll be OK with that."

The elevator door opened on the third floor and we practically spilled out onto the floor. Almost running. I felt like pushing one of them just for the heck of it. Watching us from beside a doorway was another blockman in a suit. Jesus, where did Whitey find these guys? Did they all live together? Did they hang out together when they weren't working? Lots of questions about these blockmen.

We walked toward the door. The blockman doorman opened the door, but before I could walk in, he jammed his hand against my chest, stopping me. He then thoroughly patted me down. Then we walked in. It was a big office with a window behind the desk that overlooked the club below. It was very impressive. But what was more impressive was the man behind the desk. He appeared to be in his early forties. He was a very light-skinned black man with the greenest eyes I had ever seen. I don't think his other features mattered. With that combination, he couldn't help but be good looking. I think I was taken aback and I think he was used to people being taken aback. He waited a moment before speaking, and I assumed it was so I could collect myself.

"Dean," he said as he stood and extended his hand. "Rafael here calls you Dean. I assume it is OK for me to do the same."

"Sure," I said as I shook his hand. He was not as tall as I was expecting and his handshake was not very firm. "Ralph said I should call you Whitey, is that OK?"

"Yes, yes. Let's get to the point. Rafael says that you wanted to speak to me about Jaime?"

"Yes, I do. I want you to stop looking for him. To leave him alone."

"Well," he said laughingly. "That is easier said than done. I need to find him and talk with him." He got very stern at this point. "And, if you know where he is, I expect you to tell me right now."

"I'm not certain where he is right now, but I did find him and I do have your money."

"You have my money?" he asked incredulously.

"I do and I will give most of it back to you on the condition that you leave Jaime alone. You let this one go."

"You said 'most of it.' You do not have all the money?"

"No, not all. I tried but there were expenses. I have eighty percent of it but you won't have to pay Lt. Roger or Jaime. I'll give it to you if you assure me you will never bother Jaime again. So, basically, eight million dollars to leave Jaime alone."

"Well," he laughed. "Eight million dollars. So my two choices are eight million and allow Jaime a pass or force you to tell me where the eight million is and make Jaime's life very uncomfortable. A collection attorney would charge me more than twenty percent. You located the money, are bringing it back, and simply want me to leave Jaime alone. Jaime is replaceable in my employ and I never really cared for him anyway."

"Hmm, me either," I said.

He laughed again. "It sounds as though we have a deal," he said, and he stood and reached across the desk and we shook hands again.

"Someday you need to tell me how you got this money back."

"I will," I said. "Oh, and by the way, Lt. Roger is dead."

This seemed to cause him some concern.

"Too bad. Lt. Roger will be very hard to replace and was very important. But we will figure something out. Now where is the money?" Part of me thought that maybe he thought I killed Lt. Roger. I did nothing to make him think otherwise.

"Well, if Ralph and the boys here could take me back to the Freedom Tower, I'll get it to them."

"By all means, Dean. It was very nice meeting you, and I do hope that we will meet again."

"Thank you, Whitey. I hope the same," I lied.

We walked out of there without saying anything and smushed ourselves back into the little elevator. I felt good on the way back. I hoped Whitey would be a man of his word. Jaime and, by extension, Marcia would be OK.

CHAPTER THIRTY-TWO

Ralph finally said, "How chew have this money, Dean? Is it in suitcases, a trunk, what?" It seemed as though Ralph had no idea of the size or makeup of the money, much like I had when Jaime told me he had it.

"No, Ralph, it's in six baseball equipment bags. You'll have plenty of room to put it in here," and I motioned to the rear of the Escalade.

"Cool. Chew know, Dean, Jaime and me been friends for a bery long time. Chew know. I think it is cool with Whitey if he calls me. Tell him to call me."

"I will, Ralph." I liked Ralph. Actually, I liked him more than I liked Jaime.

I had them pull behind the minivan, and we unloaded the bags. They fit in the Cadillac nicely and I shook hands with all three of them. I had written my home and Turtle phone number down for Ralph before we got to the minivan and I told them if they were ever in Amelia Island to look me up at the Turtle and I'd give them a free drink. They said they would, and I kind of had the feeling that I would see them again. Maybe I could suggest to the Ritz that they hold a blockmen convention there. Could be sponsored by companies that make wide-bodied clothing.

I got in the minivan, lit up a Chief Aquino cigar, and headed north. I knew I wasn't supposed to smoke in a rental, but what the hell? I had just done some good work and I had a long drive home. I was determined to do the drive straight through. I figured about six and half hours. I didn't want to stop at the Lago Mar. If I arrived there in this minivan, there probably would be a soccer mom convention, with my luck.

So I headed out. The sun had nearly set but I was anxious to get home and I didn't think it would be much of a drive. I found some Hispanic station that played music that was close to reggae, opened all the windows, puffed on my cigar, and hit the highway.

Fernandina was seemingly vacant when I drove through and it was quiet when I pulled in my drive. I was beat. I unloaded, stripped down to my underwear, and climbed into bed. God, there really was no place like home. I thought I'd probably sleep for days.

I slept very soundly. The next morning, I took my time, drinking coffee, listening to the music low, and generally relaxing. My phone rang around 9:00 a.m.

"Hello?"

"Dean, it's Marcia."

She sounded soft and sweet.

"Hey, Marcia, how are you?"

"I'm fine, Dean. Jaime made it here safely. He's still in bed but I wanted to call you and thank you so very much. He told me everything."

I was envisioning "everything" being Jaime singlehandedly fighting off the Dominican Army, if there is one, saving some orphans and stray dogs before flying out of the country.

"Well, good," I managed.

"He told me how you basically rescued him, saved his life, and how you took control and got us this money to start our lives over."

I was shocked. "It wasn't that big a deal, Marcia. I am glad it worked out. Tell Jaime that I talked with Whitey and all is well. He'll know what I am talking about."

"Dean, Jaime and I are going to give it another shot, but I want you to know that how very special you are to me. If that matters."

"It matters, Marcia. That's why I did it." Jesus, was I a sap.

"I know, thank you again, Dean."

"OK, Marcia, good luck." And I hung up.

Well shit, I thought. But then I thought, what the hell. Life is good and things work out like they are supposed to work out. I called Rose's cell phone number.

"Aw, mister world traveler has returned. Hopefully, to get his ass to work."

"Good morning to you, too, Rose. It's nice to be home."

"Well, what about it? You comin' in today?"

"Yeah, just wanted to let you know that I gotta return a rental car at the airport and stop at the bank and maybe a lawyer's office but I'll be there."

"OK, Dean, welcome home."

"Thanks, Rose, see you soon."

I did what I had to do that day and returned to the Turtle. As I got out of the Corvette, Butch appeared on his bike.

"Dean, knock knock."

"Butch, who's there?"

"Ho, Ho."

"Ho, ho who?"

"You're not a good Santa Claus, Dean," and he took off on his bike.

I stood there a second, watching Butch pedal away, and then went around the front of our little bar. I paused for the view. Endless ocean—this is right where I wanted to be, right now.

CHAPTER THIRTY-THREE

Everyone was there that night: Beans, Jerry, Lori, Sara, and to top it off, the next morning, while enjoying my coffee, I got flipped off by Larry Penso.

One particularly beautiful morning many days later, I was in my meditative state. I had managed to get Marcia out of my mind, and I was sitting in my rocking chair, on the deck of the Turtle, warming my face with the morning sun, when I heard her shuffling. It was Laura coming around the corner. Only her shuffling was more upbeat. She sat in the chair opposite me.

"How you doing, Laura?" I asked with my eyes closed and face to the sun.

"Wonderful, Dean, just wonderful." Enthusiastically. I opened one eye and looked at her and she smiled at me. She looked years younger.

"Good. How about a cup of coffee?"

"Perfect, Dean. Just perfect," she said, still with the youthful smile. I just looked at her and headed in to get her BeachSaver mug filled.

When I came back, her eyes were closed and her face was to the sun with a calm smile on her face. Her skin had a deep bronze tone to it, and she really was a pretty woman. She opened her eyes to take the cup and we just sat.

"Dean, do you need money?"

"Haha, no."

"If you really needed money, you would make sure you kept it or got it, right?"

"Sure, but the only money I need is for cigars. Cigar money."

"Dean, I can't stand it anymore." She was ecstatic. Almost jumping for joy.

"What?"

"The donation. Our group got an anonymous donation of one million dollars from a trust."

"Really?" I said nonchalantly.

"Yes, you don't know anything about that, do you?" she asked coyly.

"No, how would I know?"

"Because it was you" she said loud and accusingly. "I don't know how, but it was you."

"What are you talking about, Laura?"

"Haha," and she pointed at me, smiling. "The lawyer giving us the money slipped up and said the name of the trust."

"Really?" Damn lawyer.

"Yes." Her feet were curled up under her on the big rocking chair and she slowly pointed at the logo on her coffee cup. "The so-called anonymous trust giving us one million dollars, yes, one million dollars . . ." she was downright ecstatically animated now ". . . is called the BeachSaver Coffee Mug Trust."

She came over and gave me a huge hug and kiss and another hug and another kiss while she cried happy tears. It would be hard for me to think of a time I felt better. It was true: The $1 million I kept, the final baseball equipment bag, had been put in a trust I set up and then supposedly anonymously donated to Laura's cause. I didn't want the money. I believe in karma and I thought the money needed to be used for good. Maybe it was karma that money stolen by the government, then from the government, should be used to fight the government. Something like that. I really didn't need any money. All I needed was money for cigars. Just cigar money.

ABOUT THE AUTHOR

Michael and his wife live in Canton, Ohio. Michael has been a lawyer, a prosecutor, a criminal defense lawyer, an elected official, corporate counsel, an adjunct professor, an NFL agent and now a struggling writer.

Of course, he enjoys smoking cigars.